The Dime Novelist

Center Point
Large Print

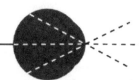

**This Large Print Book carries the
Seal of Approval of N.A.V.H.**

WEST OF THE BIG RIVER

The Dime Novelist

A Novel Based on the Life of Ned Buntline

CLAY MORE

CENTER POINT LARGE PRINT
THORNDIKE, MAINE

This Center Point Large Print edition
is published in the year 2021 by arrangement with
Western Fictioneers.

The text of this Large Print edition is unabridged.
In other aspects, this book may vary
from the original edition.
Printed in the United States of America
on permanent paper.
Set in 16-point Times New Roman type.

ISBN: 978-1-63808-153-1

The Library of Congress has cataloged this record
under Library of Congress Control Number: 2021944080

Dedicated to the memory of Edward Zane Carroll Judson, the King of the Dime Novels and of my grandfather, George Innes McDonald, who taught me how to spin a yarn

THE EAGLE'S NEST

Where the silvery gleam of the rushing stream,
Is so brightly seen o'er the rocks dark green,
Where the white pink grows by the wild red rose
And the blue bird sings till the welkin rings.

Where the red deer leaps and the panther creeps,
And the eagles scream over cliff and stream,
Where the lilies bow their heads of snow,
And the hemlocks tall throw a shade o'er all.

Where the rolling surf leaves the emerald turf,
Where the trout leaps high at the hovering fly,
Where the sportive fawn crops the soft green
  lawn,
And the crows' shrill cry bodes a tempest nigh—
There is my home—my wildwood home.

Where no step intrudes in the dense dark woods,
Here no song is heard but of breeze and bird;
Where the world's foul scum can never come;
Where friends are so few that all are true—
There is my home—my wildwood home.

Ned Buntline

Prologue

ROUGH JUSTICE

Nashville, Tennessee
March 14, 1846

The judge rapped his gavel on his desk and called for order.

"I will have silence in this court! Now pipe down all of you or I'll have the marshal and his deputies begin arresting folk."

He grunted, pushed his wire-framed spectacles further up his aquiline nose and turned his attention to the defendant sitting nonchalantly as he wrote in a small notebook at the table by the window.

"You, Mister Edward Judson, have stirred up a dust storm of trouble for yourself. If you haven't already, I would suggest you start praying that Robert Porterfield makes a full recovery, instead of scribbling away. Now put that book away and have some respect for this hearing."

Ned, for such was the sobriquet the defendant preferred to use, clicked his tongue as he quickly stowed notebook and pencil and nodded his head firmly, striving hard to put on his humblest of expressions. It was not easy for him, for "humble" was not an attitude of mind that came naturally to him. He was twenty-two years old, but had already packed several lifetimes of adventure into his short career. Or so he, as his well-known self, the writer Ned Buntline was wont to tell his readers and anyone, anywhere, whose attention he was able to grab.

He was a stocky young man of slightly less than average height with a shock of unruly red hair and a matching, fledgling mustache. Despite his relative youth his face was already weathered by sea and sun. He was wearing the Spanish cloak that he thought marked him out as the literary celebrity he considered himself to be. He had, after all, been publishing his own monthly magazine, immodestly entitled *Ned Buntline's Magazine* since 1844 and in which he oft claimed that he had won prizes for three novelettes published by three separate New York publishing houses.

Upon the table in front of him was the expensive Panama hat that so many had admired and remarked upon in the saloons, gaming parlors and stores of Nashville. Ned was not a handsome fellow, yet he never failed to attract attention. He undoubtedly had charm. He exuded it whenever he talked, especially when he addressed the members of the fairer sex.

That charm, he knew, was the underlying reason for his sorry situation in court.

"I do indeed pray for him, Your Honor," he returned. "It is not my way to harm my fellow man, but as I have said and as many here could attest to, I was provoked and I fired only in self-defense."

He stroked his mustache with the back of a finger and added: "He should have taken heed of my reputation as a crack shot."

The crowded courtroom erupted angrily, over-riding and subduing Ned's few supporters. He looked at them in surprise and alarm and immediately regretted his words. It wasn't that he meant to brag; it was simply his habit to make sure that people knew about his qualities and attributes.

The judge rapped his gavel.

"Say, where is the marshal?" he demanded of the court clerk.

The clerk looked anxiously at the judge and then at the crowd. He swallowed hard, as if his mouth had instantly gone dry as a bone. "He . . . he and his deputies slipped out about a minute ago, Judge."

Ned stiffened in his chair at this exchange. He felt the hairs on the back of his neck start to tingle, a sure sign that something was amiss.

Suddenly, the courthouse doors were thrown open and three men stomped in. They shouldered the standing onlookers out of the way and made straight towards Ned as he sat at his table.

Ned stared aghast as he recognized the leading one of the three men. It was John Porterfield, the brother of the man he had shot in the gunfight.

"You damned villain, Judson. You shot my kid brother in the head and the doc don't know if he can save him. Now I'm going to shoot you down like the dog you are."

He raised his hand and pointed the Allen & Thurber Pepperbox he was holding directly at Ned's chest. Cries rang out around the courtroom as people close by sought escape. The judge uttered a noise that could have been a cross between a profanity and a prayer and immediately ducked under his desk.

Ned, being nimble, shot to his feet, aware of the guns appearing in the other two men's hands. He saw that his own escape was barred by the seething crowd. He flashed a glance back at the Pepperbox in John Porterfield's hand and saw the bar hammer rise as he started to squeeze the trigger. A moment later there was a thunderous noise, but Ned had instinctively dodged sideward and he heard the bullet smash the window behind him. The other two men shot and missed, gouging wood from the walls. Unbridled fury had clouded their aim and caused their fists to shake as they fired.

Ned jumped upon the table, pulled his Spanish cloak off and with a swirl, hurled it at the trio of shooters. It landed over their guns and they spent a couple of seconds untangling it and throwing it aside, giving Ned time to snatch up his Panama hat and clasp it in front of his face. Then with a swift twirl on his heels he dived through the glass window.

He hit the ground outside amid shards of glass and gasped as he winded himself. Yet he ignored it as best he could, for the fusillade of bullets that pounded the dirt around him left him in no doubt that his death was mere inches and seconds away. Such situations had happened to him before and his powerful self-preservation reflexes took over. He rolled, quickly regained his feet, and ran zigzagging across the street toward an alley.

The street itself was almost deserted, for most people had eagerly crammed into the court for the hearing. Only a few drunks and loafers were about. In the corner of his vision he saw a large fellow pick up a rock and toss it at him. He ducked too late and it struck him on the head, stunning him so that he slowed and half turned to see who had tossed it. Blood poured from the wound into his eye and he staggered on. Then he heard another gunshot from the courthouse window and felt a searing pain in his chest that spun him round again.

Fortunately, his years before the mast, walking on the decks of ships tossed by storms, had given him his sea legs. He regained his balance and resumed his run. Only now there was another large figure blocking the alley entrance, ominously brandishing a club.

Ned cursed and altered direction, blood now flowing from his chest wound to soak the front of his shirt. He dashed straight over the road and entered the City Hotel. The foyer was empty so he bounded past the reception desk, along a passageway and then up the back stairs. He tested doorknobs on his way, but all were locked. Up he went to the third floor and found a vacant room. He ran in, pressed himself against the wall and pulled back his shirt to inspect his wound. Fortunately, it was merely a flesh wound, but the bullet had scored a long crease in his side which was losing more blood than he cared to lose. He did his best to staunch it with a sheet ripped off the bed. As swiftly as he could he fashioned a pad and a bandage, which he managed to wind over his clothes like a Roman toga and, in similar fashion, he tore a strip of the sheet and fashioned a bandage for his head wound.

He managed all this while he had been keeping an eye upon the window and the street below, where a crowd had formed. It was a mob with a purpose and it moved along the street, with men detaching from it and running into the various businesses and stores with much shouting and braying.

To his dismay, he saw the big fellow who had cast the rock at his head, surrounded by the Porterfield group and the marshal and his deputies.

"Those villains left the court and meant to let them shoot me down in cold blood," he mumbled to himself. "Well, at first chance, I'll outsmart all these fools and when I have secured my safety they will rue the day they crossed swords with Ned Buntline. I will sue the whole damned town, every last one of them and I shall write a true account of this day that will make the town the most despised in this great country."

Despite his dire situation his mind was already forming the story, which he had begun making notes about in the courtroom.

"There's a trail of blood!" He heard a voice from somewhere inside the hotel.

"It leads upstairs," cried another.

Heavy footfalls of running men resounded up the stairs.

Ned looked out the window and spied a horse, saddled and hitched outside the Mercantile Bank.

The noise of the pursuing pack was getting closer and he took his chance. He took two quick paces, ignoring the pain in his head and side and stepped onto the window ledge, where he balanced for long enough to launch himself for the coping above the portico. His plan was to grab it and hang from it so he could travel hand over hand and then drop down onto the saddle and make his escape. He had described such a scene countless times in some of his swash-buckling tales of agile seafaring men outwitting and escaping from lumbering landlubbers.

But in stark reality, when he tried to duplicate the adventurous leap he missed completely, bounced off the portico, rolled to its edge to fall into the dirt, winded and unable to move. He wondered at first just how many bones he must have broken, such was the pain he was in.

The mob advanced, with the elder Porterfield in the lead, his gun in his hand. But this time the marshal and his deputies were not prepared to have Ned mowed down in full sight of the town. A shot was fired into the air by the marshal and orders snapped to take Ned into custody for his own safety.

For once Ned did not even have the strength to protest. He just groaned as he was manhandled to the town jail.

A doctor saw to his wounds, stitching up both the head wound and the crease along his ribs.

"You're a lucky feller, mister," the physician said as he stowed his instruments away in his bag. "Shot in the head and in the side, yet still here to tell the tale." He gave a short laugh. "You could be a character in one of your stories. You must have a thick skull, for that rock could have crushed another man's head. And that chest wound, a couple of inches left and you would be getting measured up for a coffin right now."

"He still may if John Porterfield has his way," said Dan Grover, the deputy tasked with watching the prisoner. "The judge ain't too happy about having his courthouse fired up and the prisoner there taking off like that."

Ned shook his head. "I thank you, Doctor. But fear not, Deputy—Grover, is it?" He smiled affably and prepared to continue after the deputy gave a nod of affirmation. "In the cold light of day, when all the facts are known, the judge will dismiss this case out of hand. But now, if you wouldn't mind, I am tired and feel that I must sleep."

Indeed, as the cell door was swung closed and locked and the doctor and deputy left, Ned closed his eyes and tried to rest. He was not feeling as confident as he tried to sound, yet he did have faith in his oratorical powers and he felt that he could persuade a jury if the hearing found that a trial was needed. Although he hated the legal profession, he had read enough law books to be able to hold his own, thanks to his lawyer father's overbearing tutelage when he was a youngster.

It was, he felt, so totally unfair. True he had paid Mary, the wife of Robert Porterfield a great deal of attention. He had, in short, seduced her and been more unguarded than he should have been in keeping the short relationship secret. As for the shoot-out, Ned had been outside town practicing pistol shooting when Robert Porterfield, goaded by friends, had sought him out and immediately started shooting. He had no option but to aim and return fire.

His single shot opened a hole above Robert's right eye and he fell in a heap.

"He was lucky I did not have a proper gun," Ned whispered to himself as he drifted off into a deep sleep. "I would have blown his darned head off."

It was some hours later that the news that Robert Porterfield had died, despite two doctors' attempts at trephination by boring holes in his skull to let blood out, spread around the town like wildfire. Copious imbibing of whiskey had inflamed folks' tempers and soon another mob had formed in town.

The deputy heard them coming but left alone to guard the prisoner he feared for his own safety and made no move to stop them from breaking the door down, grabbing the keys and unlocking the cell to drag the protesting Ned out into the night.

"I demand a fair—"

"You'll get a fair death," someone yelled.

"String him up!" cried another.

A rope was tossed over an awning post in the town square and a noose was thrown round his neck and drawn tight. Ned fought as best he could but he was punched and gouged, and his hands were forced behind his back and tied tight.

Still protesting, the rope was pulled by many hands and Ned felt himself hauled off his feet, dragged by his neck and left dangling several feet above the ground.

He felt himself choking, his vision went red and he could hear nothing but the cheers of glee and gloating of the mob. He was sure that somewhere among them he heard John Porterfield laugh and, he fancied, a woman was crying.

Then he heard no more.

How long he was left hanging he did not know, nor did the three generous friends who cut him down as soon as the mob broke up and drifted away to the various watering holes about town.

Fear that Nashville would be branded a town that lynched men without a trial undoubtedly swayed the judge, so he ordered that a grand jury should be assembled some days later. With his throat, head and chest heavily bandaged, Ned was given his day in court. He managed to get witnesses to the shooting and his plea of self-defense was grudgingly accepted and no indictment was found against him.

Ned left town quietly and duly gave an account in *Ned Buntline's Magazine* of his wrongful arrest and bold escape. It was the sort of tale that his readers had grown accustomed to and many a young man would root for the noble author as they read the latest enthralling account of Ned Buntline's seemingly charmed and adventurous life. And if any of these readers was fortunate enough to meet the great man in later years and ask him about the veracity of his adventures, they would be greeted with a firm hand on the shoulder, a beaming smile and the rejoinder:

"Sir, I am a man of honor and just as my tongue would twist itself into a knot rather than tell a lie, so too my pen is only able to fashion a story from the truth."

Even from his earliest years Ned believed that he had immense potential within him. He also believed that great men were permitted to bend the truth and that the bent truth, once in print, stayed in print and thereby was proof of the truth.

"Someday," he promised himself, once his wounds had healed and his pride was intact again, "I will find a chronicler to record my life's stories. The world deserves to know about my adventurous life. An official biographer, that is what I need."

LETTER FROM E. Z. C. JUDSON
The Eagle's Nest
March 12, 1881

My Dear Frederick, or rather, Fred (as I see you tend to use the abbreviated form in your writings!)

I will, if you do not object, use your Christian name, for after reading the two editions of your most excellent journal *Turf, Field and Farm*, containing your editorials and several of your most entertaining articles I feel that I know you already.

I was honored by your invitation to contribute an article on trout fishing and have enclosed a short anecdote which you may wish to publish.

As to your suggestion that I might grant you an interview in order to write an article about my life, I am flattered in the extreme. However, most who know me well will testify to my innate sense of propriety and modesty. At first, I was tempted to reply in the negative, but upon careful consideration, I have decided to come back with a different proposal.

Many of my readers have written to

me asking that I should pen an auto-biographical account of my life. I have always scoffed at the idea, until your letter had an Archimedean effect upon me. Eureka! I cried as I took my morning bath.

So, good Fred, my proposal is that instead of a short interview, you come and stay for a couple of days at the Eagle's Nest. Perhaps you could then return in a month or so, which will give you time to write and then come up with more questions. An autobiography resounds with arrogance, but a series of biographical sketches written by a literate author of Boswellian talent, such as your good self would be sure to find a following among the readers of my humble works.

If this appeals in any way, then do please write back.

I am, your humble and obedient servant,
Edward Zane Carroll Judson (Colonel)

NOTEBOOK 1

Property of Fred E. Pond
Private & Confidential

JOTTINGS ON THE LIFE OF NED BUNTLINE
April 1881

Note 1
Received a reply from Colonel Judson. He has invited me to stay at his home, Eagle's Nest!
I wrote back eagerly in the affirmative. I am to write a series of biographical sketches!

Note 2
This little notebook is for my sole use and will contain thoughts and snippets of information and areas that I must pursue as we progress.

Note 3
I am conscious of the privilege it is going to be to meet Colonel Edward Zane Carroll Judson and his wife Anna at their home, The Eagle's Nest in Stamford. In taking on this role as his chronicler I am conscious of my limitations as a writer but am hopeful that I can do this great man's life justice.

Note 4
My first task will be to get an overall impression
of the colonel's home and glean some impression
of his early years.

Chapter 1

A WRITER'S RETREAT

The Eagle's Nest, Stamford,
April, 1881

Colonel Edward Judson, better known throughout the land by his writing pen name of Ned Buntline, was in a reflective mood. Over the preceding two months he had fought off a threatened bout of melancholia following the sudden death of Irene, his beloved four-year-old daughter after an illness of just two days. He had done so in his usual phlegmatic manner, by immersing himself in local affairs, planning a temperance lecture tour in the summer and writing countless devotional poems. The Washington's Birthday celebrations in February had gone superbly to plan with the town band escorting Ned from the Eagle's Nest to Hamilton House for a feast, innumerable toasts and his ever-eloquent speech in honor of George Washington and Abraham Lincoln. Then, after darkness when he returned home he lit up the valley below with a fireworks display that eclipsed the ones he habitually gave on the Fourth of July.

Now, as the snows had receded, and the sap

was rising in the trees he had decided it was time to return to serious novel writing. The only thing that hampered him was pain.

His many old wounds and injuries, all of which he had referred to in *Beadle & Adams* or *Street & Smith* dime novels, or any number of magazine articles and essays, had been troubling him for several days, provoked he was sure by the gout which reared its leviathan head whenever he over-imbibed in the moonshine corn mash whiskey he had Old Abner, one of his hunting companions from the Adirondacks send to him by the caseload. Ever the patriot, he held to his principle of never drinking Scotch or Irish whiskey, no matter how expensive, old or good they were claimed to be. He had no patience with foreigners or their goods.

He was a stocky fellow a shade under average height and a touch more than average weight, with a mane of red hair peppered with strands of silver, a weather-beaten face and a thick, red walrus mustache. He was dressed in his favorite writing clothes, which consisted of buckskins, moccasins and a floppy hunting hat with a hawk's feather stuck in the band.

Ned had built the Eagle's Nest in 1871 at a cost of $25,000. It lay deep in the Hudson Highlands, overlooking the Delaware Valley and successive Catskill ranges, and had been erected in honor of the hunting lodge that he had loved so much when he was a younger and more carefree man. It was surrounded by one hundred and twenty acres of game preserve, where he could shoot and hunt to his heart's delight.

Literary success had provided him with the means to indulge himself and his beloved wife, Anna, whom he called Hazel Eyes. It had also given him enough to pay off four of his other previous wives, with the exception of Lovanche, who it seemed was determined to hound him through the courts and whatever other way she could muster until his dying day.

Whereas the original Eagle's Nest in the Adirondacks was little more than a trapper's cabin, the Stamford dwelling was a veritable mansion, built as Colonel Judson deemed to be necessary for one of his considerable prestige. It had a large conservatory and multiple rooms decorated in the latest and most luxurious fashions, as suited Hazel Eyes. In addition, it had a smoking room, a gun room and a huge study, which she left to Ned to furnish however he wished.

In his present state of infirmity the great writer was restricted to hobbling between the gun room, which he called "the armory," where he kept his guns, his fishing rods and his collection of medieval swords, crossbows, bows and arrows, and his study, bedecked with portraits of the many illustrious characters of the West that he had known, or whom he had made famous after including them in one or more of his eagerly awaited dime novels. Two walls were covered with high bookcases stacked with books on all manner of subjects. One of them was devoted exclusively to novels, magazines and stories in pamphlet form that he had written himself.

Ned Buntline was, in short, the famed King of the Dime Novels; the man who had produced, edited and published countless magazines, including *Ned Buntline's Magazine*, *Ned Buntline's Own*, *Ned Buntline's Novelist*, and *The Patriot's Banner*, and who had authored over five hundred dime novels under his main writer's sobriquet of Ned Buntline and over a dozen other pen names, including Captain Cleighmore, Harrison Gray Buchanan, Jiles Edwards and one he was especially fond of—"Mad Jack." At a conservative estimate, he earned around $20,000 a year from his work with the publishers *Street & Smith* and several more thousand from his dime novels with *Beadle & Adams*.

He was sitting at his great oak desk, which was littered as usual with his writing paraphernalia, his pipe rack, a cigar box and piles of books and papers and a few framed photographs. He was smoking his favorite corncob pipe and contemplating the direction he was going to take his latest story about *Merciless Bill, the Hair Lifter*, which he was penning in installments for Street & Smith's *New York Weekly*.

"What'll it be, Ned," he thought to himself. "A touch of satire, a gentle political jibe at Roscoe Conkling, or just a straightforward tale of Merciless Bill beating the hell out of the crooked Indian agent and lifting his scalp in retribution for his rape of the dead chief's squaw?"

Although he liked others to address him as Colonel Judson, when he retreated into his own mind he liked to be just plain Ned Buntline, the gifted storyteller who could chat to anyone. Thus, he kept up a dialogue with himself, which no one else was privy to, apart from in the stories or poems that were the inevitable result of his inner musings.

"Damn it, I am in no mood for politics in this one, let it just be straightforward adventure."

And with a puff of satisfaction he blew a stream of blue smoke toward the rafters and then clamping the pipe betwixt his teeth, he picked up a quill, dipped it in the ornate inkpot made from a horn of a buffalo he had himself shot back before the war, and then he began to write.

His pen scratched out beautiful copperplate words at a great rate, back and forth across the paper for an hour as the characters darted about, fought, drank and fought again in multi-colored images in his mind.

He stood up abruptly in mid paragraph, lay down the long gone cold corncob pipe in the ashtray and hobbled round the desk to pick up his stick. It was an ebony shaft with a heavy ivory handle in the shape of a tomahawk, which had been his companion in many an adventure, both in imagination and in reality.

With the tomahawk grip in his right hand he pulled on the shaft with his left and swiftly drew out the hidden sword within. Then tossing the sheath on the leather chair:

"Have at you, Frobisher, you son of a dog, I'll teach you how we deal with vermin," he cried, as he swished the sword, then executed a series of fencing moves as he acted the part of Merciless Bill confronting the Indian agent. "Take that, and that—and that!"

His voice rose ever higher as he thrust, parried and lunged across the study floor. Then, landing his foot as he made a final lunge with the sword in the direction of the door, he felt a stab of pain in his gouty foot and he yelled.

"Gah! That did it! I'm dead!"

And he fell writhing on the floor.

Suddenly, the door was thrown open by Anna, his beautiful wife, whose blue eyes flecked with brown and corn yellow hair always reminded him of an angel and whom he always referred to affectionately as Hazel Eyes when they were in private. Her angelic eyes suddenly looked aghast and full of concern to see her husband in such pain.

"Oh Edward, my goodness, we thought you had been attacked."

"Attacked, I'm always under attack with this blamed foot, my love. But why in tarnation did you say 'we'?"

The thin face of a young man in pebble-thick metal framed spectacles peered over her shoulder.

"That . . . that would be because of me, sir. Fred Pond at your service."

He looked nervously into the study and spied the sword still clasped in Ned's hand. "Has . . . has your attacker escaped, Colonel? Should I summon an officer of the law?"

Ned tossed his head back and gave a hearty laugh. Then: "I'm attacked by gout, sir. But it shall not overcome me. Give me a hand up and let's have a look at each other."

Anna rushed in and took one arm and was about to haul, when he withdrew his arm.

"No, my love, not in your condition," he said, gently patting the prominent bump. "Take care of my little son, there."

Fred Pond swiftly interceded and taking his other arm pulled Ned to his feet.

"This is a great honor, Colonel Judson, sir. I am here armed with notebooks and ready to begin. Where should I put my bags?"

Ned hobbled over to the chair and sheathed his swordstick. He turned and leaned heavily on it, staring pugnaciously up at the young man, who stood at least four inches taller than him. "Bags, sir? What do you mean, where should you put them?"

Who is this interloping popinjay who looks in need of a good feed, he thought.

Anna shook her head in exasperation. "Edward, you really should pay attention. This is Mister Frederick Pond, the journalist who is here to stay with us for a few days. You arranged it yourself."

Ned pushed his hat up on his head, allowing a cascade of unruly red hair to tumble free.

"I did?" He pointed his stick at the chair. "Then sit, Mister Pond and remind me. I have been somewhat distracted of late."

Anna gave a wan smile as Fred Pond eagerly sat down. "We had a family tragedy, but we are doing quite well," she said by way of explanation for her husband's behavior. "I shall bring coffee."

"A tragedy? Oh my," Fred returned. "Then I shouldn't intrude. I . . . I—"

Ned waved a hand at him. "Life plays cruel tricks on us all, I am afraid. We lost a child, but we are comforted in knowing that she is smiling as she looks down on us from heaven. Think no more about it, good sir."

Anna nodded and smiled emphatically and reassuringly. "Really, my husband is quite right. She smiles, so we carry on. Now, I am sure that you will benefit from a cup of coffee, as will Edward, after his tumble."

"You are an angel, Hazel Eyes," replied Ned. Then with a smile at Fred:

"And now sir—ah, you have a letter? It is an introduction from one of my publishers, I take it?"

Fred Pond smiled nervously. "Not exactly, sir. It is an invitation that you wrote to me yourself."

Ned sat down in the other leather chair and eased his gouty foot onto the footstool.

"Ah yes, excuse me," he said as he scanned the letter. "Of course, you are the Fred E. Pond, who writes under the name of Will Wildwood. I sent you my little essay about—about—"

"You wrote about trout fishing, sir. Actually, we have corresponded several times, since then. You were very flattering about my book—"

"Indeed!" said Ned, striving hard to recollect what they had corresponded about. Often he had to indulge in such conversational "fishing" for clues, a consequence of having written letters when he was under the influence of old Abner's moonshine. "And your book, the title of which escapes me momentarily—"

"There are two, Colonel, I sent them both to you. *Poems of the Rod and Gun* and *The Sportsman's Directory and Yearbook.*" He pulled off his spectacles and breathed on the lenses preparatory to polishing them, a habit he had developed when talking about his books. Fred

Pond was twenty-five years of age and had left the West for New York in order to take over the editorship of *Turf, Field and Farm* and to try and build a literary career. He was short-sighted, wiry in build and with a clean-shaven but wholesome face.

"And excellent works they are both. I read them cover to cover," Ned lied, having no recollection of them whatsoever. Indeed, he only vaguely remembered the fishing article.

"That's praise indeed, coming from you, Colonel. You are, if I may say so, an utter inspiration to myself and to thousands of other beginning writers."

That was the sort of flattery that went straight to Ned's heart. He could take any amount of it and always treated the flatterer with respect, as though receiving compliments was the last thing in the world that he expected.

"I am merely an old wordsmith trying to tell a tale, give a little entertainment and hopefully every now and then I succeed in enlightening people," he said with a self-deprecating smile.

"No sir, you are a literary lion and I have read maybe eighty or so of the dime novels you have written. I read my first one when I was eight years old and ever since then it has been my ambition to follow the path you have trodden, Colonel. The path in your literary life that is, rather than the actual adventures, for you have crammed more living into your life than any ten men."

"It is true, Mister Pond, I have had a full life, but I am no lion. Merely a scribbler."

"Oh please, call me Fred. You may recall that when you wrote to me you indicated that you would call me Fred?"

"Absolutely. Of course I did and so Fred it shall be. And I suppose therefore, you should call me Edward." He grinned. "Or perhaps, just Ned."

Fred Pond looked amazed and he grinned and opened his mouth to speak, before snapping it shut and clenching his jaw with some determination. Then he spoke hesitantly, as if fearful of offending the great writer. "Actually, if it would be all right with you I would rather address you as Colonel. It seems right and proper to maintain your rank, sir."

His eye fell on the photograph of Ned's younger self on a corner of the desk. He pointed to it in some excitement. "You see, sir. That picture is how the world thinks of you. As a veteran of the war and a distinguished soldier."

In the picture Ned was dressed in the uniform of a colonel of the US Army, resplendent with numerous medals pinned to his chest.

Fred's excited expression turned to one of dawning realization and he took a sharp intake of breath. "I swear I have seen a photograph of President Abraham Lincoln himself in that chair."

"You have sharp eyes, Fred. It was Abe's chair," Ned avowed with a nod.

"In . . . Incredible," stammered Fred in obvious awe. Then he pointed excitedly to the photograph beside it, of Ned dressed in buckskins standing beside a seated younger man, who was immediately recognizable as Buffalo Bill Cody. On Cody's other side was a taller, similarly dressed scout, the famous Texas Jack Omohundro.

He whistled like a youngster seeing his heroes before him. "Or like that. As a chief of scouts with two other famous scouts."

Ned grinned and waved his hands in self-deprecating acceptance. He liked being called Colonel and used the title whenever he could, even though it had been decades since he actually held a military rank. In fact, the highest rank he ever attained was that of sergeant, but even then, he had been broken back to corporal for drunkenness on duty, during the Civil War. He had enlisted in the First New York Mounted Rifles, in which he became Sergeant of K Company. When he was demoted he surreptitiously "borrowed" Colonel Charles Cleveland Dodge, his commanding officer's uniform and sought out Mathew Brady's Photographer's Studio in Washington to have his portrait taken. It was purely luck that he should find himself sitting in the same chair as the president had used, but it was one he had capitalized on many times over the ensuing years.

When he finally left the army, he assumed the title and used the photograph as evidence. No one had ever questioned him on his use of the title, for he used it frequently in his tales of derring-do which featured himself as the hero.

Looking at the photograph now he thought of how different things could have been if he had been busted from Sergeant a year later, because by then Dodge would have been promoted to the rank of Brigadier General at the age of twenty-two. Ned would have liked to assume that rank, but even he had to admit to himself it might have been a lie too far.

"I really cannot thank you enough for inviting me here to the Eagle's Nest for a whole week to give me material for the biography," Fred enthused. "I have the title planned already."

"Ah, yes, the biography," Ned repeated. "You flatter me, Fred."

"I mean to tell the world about your great contributions, Colonel. We know much about you through your many dime novels. And you introduced us to the likes of Colonel William Cody and Wild Bill Hickok. It is only fitting that someone should try to do the same for you. Even if it is just a writer of meager talent, such as I."

Ned waved his hand dismissively. "No, Fred, you do yourself an injustice. I have read your work and know your literary talent, remember. I am sure you will do a fine job."

In truth, Ned was not sure that he relished someone else telling his biography. Yet it was a fait accompli, it seemed. He himself had somehow invited this scholarly young man into his home to do it. He decided therefore, to make sure that he presented him in as well rounded a manner as possible, to portray himself as a soldier, Indian fighter, bounty hunter, scholar, philanthropist and loving family man.

"The title, then. Let us have it, Fred."

Just then Anna pushed open the door and came in with a silver coffee service.

"You are just in time to hear the title of the biography that young Fred is going to write, my angel."

He gestured to Fred. "Tell us, my boy."

"It is unpretentious and is simply this, Colonel. *Life of Ned Buntline.*"

Anna clapped her hands. "Capital."

Ned, however, looked slightly crestfallen, but after a moment's thought he snapped his fingers. "Why not pepper that up just a smidgeon, my boy. May I suggest *Life and Adventures of Ned Buntline?*"

Fred took a rapid intake of breath. "But of course, this must be a book that truly tells your part in American history. You as one of the nation's supreme adventurers."

Ned beamed. "I agree, although 'supreme' is perhaps overstating the mark. Perhaps 'best-loved' would be homelier, a little more in keeping with my meager popularity as a novelist and chronicler of history." He clapped his hands. "Why, I am suddenly consumed with enthusiasm, Fred. So, let us sup coffee and then let us begin."

Chapter 2

EARLY DAYS

For two days Fred Pond followed Ned about like a lapdog, making copious notes as the great writer rambled on, recounting tales of his past in no particular order. The young scribe jotted everything down, intent upon unscrambling his thoughts later on and laying them down in a chronological order.

"I think my mother, God rest her dear soul, knew that I was destined to have a tempestuous nature and lead a turbulent life," Ned informed Fred over his shoulder as he hobbled along, searching for a book in the vast bookcases.

"Why so, Colonel?" Fred asked from the leather chair that he had grown so accustomed to, pencil at the ready.

"Because my entry into the world was not easy for her. I was a large baby, but the main reason was that she went into labor as a tempest swept over the mountains and along the valley. Lightning flashed, and thunder crashed, as if the great god Thor himself was riding a chariot across the heavens. In fact, I wrote a poem about it some years ago."

"Is it published in one of your poetry collections, Colonel?"

"Of course it is, my boy," Ned returned, without stopping his search. "But it is also published in here," he said, lifting his writing hat and tapping his prodigious forehead, which was creased with a singular scar. "All of my poems are emblazoned on my memory."

"I don't suppose—"

"That you could hear it? Of course, young Fred. It goes like this:

"Born when tempests wild were raging
O'er the earth, athwart the sky,
When mad spirits seemed as waging
Battle fierce for mast'ry:
Born when thunder loudly booming
Shook the roof above my head—
When red lightning lit the glooming
Which o'er the land and sea was spread."

Indeed, as he recited it, Ned could almost see the forks of lightning and the peals of thunder that he had been told rang out across the valley as rain hammered on the roof as he was born. When his mother had told him about it when he was old enough to remember such tales, he himself concluded that the tempest was an omen. He felt sure that the divine had implanted the seeds of greatness within him. That greatness, he believed, would carry him through many adventures and give him the lightning fast imagination and wit to succeed in whatever area of life he chose to follow.

His eyes glistened when he finished the recitation, which he had delivered with his full oratorical and thespian fervor. It worried him not a jot if it came over as melodramatic or self-aggrandizing.

"She was a lovely woman, the finest and gentlest mother that ever a young lad could wish for. And what a marvelous imagination she had. My earliest recollections were of her sitting me on her knee and making up yarns."

"Fascinating. So, your imagination came from her?"

"Indubitably, young Fred. She could make up a story like that," he said with a snap of his fingers. "Even though she was not given to writing. She had beautiful handwriting, mind you, it was just that she only ever wrote when sending letters to her family."

"Your father, then. Was he a writer and was he also blessed with imagination?"

"Indeed, he was a writer, but as for imagination, he had little. You see, he was a lawyer in his later years and a passionate student of the Revolutionary War, upon which subject he penned two tomes. He was a self-taught lawyer and had been the principal of Beech Woods

Academy at Bethany in Pennsylvania for a while when I was very young, although I scarcely remember it at all. Most of my early memories come from a homestead he bought on Dyberry Creek."

"And was he a gentle soul, like your mother?"

Ned looked over his shoulder and shook his head with a grimace. "He was anything but gentle, Fred. Levi Carroll Judson—'tis a family tradition to use the middle name Carroll, by the way. I am Edward Zane Carroll Judson, you see—but as I was saying, my father was a firm believer in discipline. He modeled himself upon our Puritan forefathers. He used to proudly boast that Judsons were among the very first of the Pilgrim Fathers to sail out from Plymouth." He sighed and clicked his tongue. "From my earliest days he laid down rules for my sister and I to follow."

"He was stern?"

"He did not spare the rod, Fred. This old body of mine has a multitude of scars from old wounds, but the earliest of them are from my father. He would beat me for misdemeanors, but in that he probably did little different from other fathers of that time. He never beat me so badly that I was seriously scarred."

"But I thought you just said that—?"

"He left me with scars, yes, but they were scars in the mind, not on the body. But I get slightly ahead of myself and I shall come to this presently. As you may see, I have been distracted by this search of my bookcase, which sadly has been to no avail."

He straightened up and with his tomahawk-handled swordstick outstretched pointed to the door. "Come Fred, I need to show you the armory."

Fred entered the room ahead of Ned and stood looking about in wonder. It was the domain of a hunter. One wall was taken up with the heads of mountain lions, antelopes and even a couple of buffalo. A huge 600 pound stuffed grizzly bear stood in menacing pose, as if about to charge. Glass cases took up a large part of another wall, all full of various types of stuffed fish.

There were gun racks, fishing racks full of all manner of rods, cases full of fishing flies, and racks of swords.

"Incredible, Colonel. You must have shot all manner of creature. Have you hunted big game abroad? Like in Africa or India?"

Ned gave one of his deep belly laughs. "I have hunted and fished all over this great country and I keep the taxidermists busy. I have sailed the southern seas and I love the oceans, yet my heart is here on the land now. It is my considered opinion that it is the greatest place on earth and I have no wish to cross the great ocean to see Britain, Europe or Africa. I think that those countries have people enough and that is where they should all stay. America is for Americans, Fred. That is my firm assertion. That is why wherever I go, wherever I stay, I fly Old Glory from my window, so that everyone can tell that I am a patriot."

"I saw it flying from your flagpole when I arrived, Colonel."

Fred turned his attention to the other side of the room, which was a veritable museum. There was a small cannon in the corner, with three metal cannonballs alongside it. Beside it was a suit of armor.

"The cannon works," Ned said, divining the question that was on Fred's mind. "I fire it three times a year. Every Washington Day, every 4th of July and on the stroke of midnight every New Year's Eve. Of course, not with cannonball, just with gunpowder and a few clods of earth. And the suit of armor is also genuine. It is an English sixteenth century jousting suit. It weighs about one hundred pounds and when you wear it, you can barely move, as it is designed to keep you immobile upon a strong steed."

He smiled and tapped the side of his nose in conspiratorial fashion. "I have an agent who is trying to negotiate the purchase of a combat suit from Spain for me, Fred. The British think that they were the masters of armor-making, just as they think they are the masters of everything, but the Spanish knew how to make steel. A good Spanish steel sword would slice through English armor nine times out of ten."

Fred nodded and made a mental note to explore at an opportune moment whether Ned actually had an antipathy toward the British.

"And here I have Scottish claymores, Samurai swords, a battle-axe, a mace and a two-handed sword that must have been wielded by a giant of a man. Someone like that Scottish hero, William Wallace."

"Weapons are a passion for you, aren't they, Colonel?"

"They are and I am a student of history, as you will have noted from my novels."

Ned pointed to a table upon which were a series of assorted whips.

"That bullwhip I won in a game of poker in Deadwood from Martha Jane Canary, whom the world knows as Calamity Jane, thanks in no small measure to my dime novel about her, *Calamity Jane and the Crooked Trail Robbers*. It was I who gave her the name, *Calamity,* if you didn't know."

For a moment his mind drifted back through the years, to the dalliances he had with Jane and of the skills she had demonstrated with a riding quirt. The poker game he referred to had only two players and the stakes weren't exactly penny ante.

He beamed at Fred as he quickly shoved the memory of the scantily clad Calamity Jane standing over him, tapping her quirt against her palm. He coughed as he regained his composure.

"But it wasn't that, which I wanted to show you, Fred. It was this!"

He picked up a thick leather man's belt.

"This was the weapon that my father used to chastise me for playing truant and for hunting and fishing instead of reading the books he foisted upon me. And for fighting with other boys."

"I know that you have had many battles, Colonel, but have you always been a fighting man?"

Again, Ned laughed as he thwacked the belt against the table with a resounding noise. "For all that you may have heard about me, my good Fred, I am not a belligerent man. I hardly ever started a fight, but I oft finished them. No, even as a callow young lad I was not an aggressor, but a defender of those less able than myself, and a defender of virtue and principles."

He laid the leather belt down again. "If my father found that I had been in a fight, whether from a black eye or a cut or grazed knuckle, he would order me to the woodshed and give me the belt. I always accepted it, because he was my father, even though I regarded it as unjust. And as later life proved, it was ineffective as a deterrent, for I spent a great deal of my life fighting."

Fred made a note in his book, and then pursed his lips. "What sort of books did he foist on you?"

"Ah, perhaps I am harsh to use that word. The truth is that I was always fond of books and would read any sort of publication given to me. No, he had a desire to make me a lawyer like himself, so he gave me legal books to read, such as *Blackstone and Coke*. Dry tomes they were, too, for I had other things I wanted to do. Whenever I had the chance, I would skip school or chores to go fishing or hunting. Yet I have to admit that my father was not totally against such activities, for at the age of eight years, after I had learned to shoot with his old gun, he gave me my very own rifle. Of course, when I appeared at breakfast the following morning after leaving the house to try out my weapon at sunup, my parents were horrified to see blood on my hands."

"You had shot yourself?" Fred asked with open mouth.

"No, Fred. That I have never done. I had in fact killed a doe with one clean shot. I did not have the strength to carry it home. I had thought that my father would be impressed, but other than ordering me to clean myself, he returned his attention to his bacon and eggs and the notes he had by his side. He was preoccupied with an article on Freemasonry that he was writing at that time."

"So he was a Freemason?"

"Absolutely. And a dangerous time it was, too. An Anti-Masonic party had been started shortly before, which opposed the secret rituals of the Freemasons. Indeed, you may remember that William Morgan, a resident of Batavia wrote a treatise exposing Masonic secrets, after which he was arrested and then went missing. It was thought that Freemasons had murdered him. That really fueled the movement against the Freemasons. I have to tell you, Fred that I as an eight-year-old lad experienced the backlash, since it was well known in Dyberry Creek that my father was a Freemason."

Ned stared into the distance, a habit that Fred had already noticed when he was deep into his anecdotage. It was as if he was looking back through time and seeing himself, which was indeed the case.

"I was on my own, walking back from a neighbor's house one evening as it started to get dark. I was stopped by a gang of boys, some two or three years older than I who started jeering at me and called me 'Lousy Mason.' Then they pelted me with stones. I was terrified, thinking that mayhap they might stone me to death and leave me in a ditch. So, I ran for my life and to the safety of my home.

"My father questioned me as to why I was so out of breath and so flushed. Then he saw the bruises from the stoning on my legs and arms and he flew into a rage about me fighting. I said nothing about them calling me Lousy Mason, for I feared that he might go out and get into an argument or fight with Anti-Masons and get himself killed. So, I accompanied him to the woodshed for another chastisement and meeting with our old friend, the leather belt there."

Fred whistled softy. "And it left another scar upon your mind."

"It did, but I resolved in my own mind that if he ever did so again, I would disown him."

Fred spluttered. "You . . . you would disown your father?"

Ned nodded emphatically. "That is what I said. But the next couple of years I pretty well did what was expected of me. I studied at school, I did chores and attended Sunday school. In my free time, though, I fished and hunted. I learned how to tie trout flies—which as you can see, I still do myself," he said, pointing to the case full of different specimens and the table with a mounted magnifying glass, a fine vice and all the other paraphernalia of the fly-fisherman's craft. "I loved my life there in Dyberry Creek and when out in the great open, hunting rabbit or deer, or fishing in the creeks, I let my imagination wander freely. I made up tales for my own amusement and fully intended that when I grew up I should be another Daniel Boone."

"It sounds an idyllic time for you, apart from your father's strict discipline."

"It was, Fred, until my father decided that we should move to Philadelphia, so that he could build up a law practice. My mother and sister fell in with him, of course, for he was the head of the family, but I saw nothing to commend the prospect. I loved the wide-open spaces, the mountains, trees and rivers and all the flowers and animals that I could admire, chase or hunt. I told him so, to no avail. He was determined that we should all go and that when I was there I should truly start preparing myself to follow him into the law. And so, all our household belongings were loaded into a wagon and we set off for the city."

Fred Pond tapped his notebook. "Yet it must have been exciting, Colonel. I come from the West and I still can hardly get used to the thrill of New York. There cannot be a place like it in my opinion. Philadelphia must surely have had a similar effect on you as a youngster, sir?"

Ned slumped into a chair beside the stuffed grizzly bear and stroked his chin. He pulled out an old yellow oilskin tobacco pouch from a pocket of his buckskin coat and began charging the corncob pipe with thick-cut tobacco. "It was an elegant place, right enough. The houses in the squares were made of bricks and were shaded by trees. The sidewalks were pristine clean and everywhere there were fine folks in fancy clothes, horse-drawn carriages and buggies. There were servants in livery scrubbing marble steps, washing windows and carrying bundles of shopping for their wealthy mistresses.

"Our own house on Girard Square, off Chestnut Street seemed huge to me. It had a study where Father locked himself away to study or to write articles, which he sent off to all manner of magazines and publishers. Philadelphia was, you see, the publishing capital of the country. Or so Father used to tell me."

He struck a light to his pipe and puffed it into life, eerily surrounding the huge stuffed bear in wreathes of blue smoke.

"When Father was not about I wandered around the streets just as I had wandered around the hills and the woods of Dyberry Creek. I got to know them, and I became familiar with the people, their houses and their servants. And then wonder of wonders I came across the Chestnut Street Theater!"

Fred noticed how his eyes glowed as he mentioned it. "Ah, the theater, it has certainly been a large part of your life, hasn't it, Colonel?"

"Indeed, Fred. I love the theater in all of its

forms. I like plays, magic acts, juggling and all form of singing entertainments. I enjoy circus, fire-eating, strong man acts and trapeze artists. I have seen them all and I have of course, in my time been a member of medicine shows, light entertainments and plays in some of the most fashionable theaters and entertainment halls in the country."

He winked at Fred. "And many of the least salubrious saloons and back alley dives, too!"

He pointed to a small valise beside the wall. "Now that we are on the subject of the theater, in that case I have various artifacts that were given to me by The Great Olivetti, a magician, juggler and ventriloquist. I came across him when I was twenty years old and saved him from being run out of a Kansas cowtown. In thanks, he taught me enough to give a passable magic show myself, which in later life I used before our stage shows. If you will just pick it up and bring it here."

Fred rose and picked up the valise, upon which were various travel stickers and gummed on playbills advertising *Scouts of the Prairies*, and *Scouts of the Plains* and various other shows. He crossed toward Ned, holding the case out.

Suddenly, from the case a voice cried out. "Help! Let me out!"

Fred gasped and dropped the case in shock. "What . . . what on earth?"

Ned laughed. "Forgive me, Fred. I could

not resist showing off a little ventriloquism. Throwing the voice is a skill that has stood me in good stead on many occasions." He bent down and picked up the case and rested it on his knee. He flicked the latch and opened it to pick out a wooden doll dressed in cream colored, elaborately fringed range clothes and a flamboyant Stetson. It had a comedic face with a goatee beard and mustache. Ned inserted his hand inside it and sat it on top of the case so that its jointed legs dangled over the edge. He worked its mouth from inside.

"Well how do, Mister Frederick Pond," the doll seemed to say. "It is an honor to meet you, sir. I hope that you are enjoying your stay with my old friend, Ned Buntline, here."

Fred chuckled. "Why it is Buffalo Bill Cody! That is marvelous, Colonel."

The Buffalo Bill puppet turned its head toward the valise. "Are you coming out here, too Wild Bill?" he called.

There was a muffled reply from the case. "I will if'n that Buntline feller isn't showing off playing cards. I had me a bellyful of his tricks."

Buffalo Bill turned to Ned. "Why don't you call him, Colonel?"

Ned shook his head. "Maybe another time, Buffalo Bill."

The puppet nodded and called out, "The colonel is busy, Bill. He says another time."

"Suits me," came back the muffled retort.

Fred Pond could not restrain himself. He applauded with enthusiasm. "Phenomenal, Colonel. You have a gift indeed. A perfect illusion there."

Ned grinned as the puppet Cody bowed. With a laugh he stowed the puppet away again. "Maybe another time I'll introduce you to Buffalo's sidekick. He's a bit temperamental, though and likes to fire his guns whenever there is an audience." He winked. "You will appreciate that I don't want to alarm my Hazel Eyes with gunfire in her present condition."

He took out a conjuror's wand from the case and waved it theatrically. "This was The Great Olivetti's very own wand. It is made of ebony with ivory tips. Observe!"

And holding it by its ends he slowly separated his hands to leave the wand floating in midair.

Fred clapped his hands again "Excellent, Colonel."

"That's not all," Ned said, replacing the wand and taking out a pack of playing cards, which he proceeded to riffle and perform a succession of sleights. "This is what Wild Bill Knicknock, as I call my Hickok puppet in the valise, was referring. Whenever I have been invited to gamble, I merely do a few of these tricks, perhaps deal off four aces at will, then ask whether they dare to play with me. It has saved me from losing money over the green cloth, for gambling is not one of my favorite pastimes."

His mind again conjured up the memory of Calamity Jane all covered in soapsuds in a Deadwood hotel bathtub, with a wet poker spread of cards in her hands as he prepared to call her bluff.

Fred misinterpreted the smile that had formed on Ned's face. "I can see that fooling gamblers would be child's play for you, Colonel. I have read several of your humorous *Beauregard Lockhart the Riverboat Gambler* dime novels. In your *Raw Deal on the Mississippi* you had Beauregard do just that series of tricks, if I am not mistaken."

Ned replaced the deck of cards in the case and guffawed. "Quite correct, Fred. And my little Buffalo Bill ventriloquist doll there, was made by a toymaker in Cincinatti. I had it made when we were performing there in *Scouts of the Plains* and I used my conjuring tricks and a bit of puppet work to amuse the kids before the curtains proper went up. Afterwards, I kept them as a reminder to myself that I made Bill Cody the legend that he is today. It was my descriptions of him in my tales that led to his fame."

He sighed. "And I did the same for James Butler Hickok, as well. So I could not resist having a puppet made of him too. I have amused children and adults at countless gatherings over the years, but I confess that hearing Wild Bill

54

Knicknock's voice, that's the name I used for the puppet, often even brings me to tears."

With a shrug he struck a light and puffed his pipe, watching the wisps of smoke drifting upwards. It seemed to Fred Pond that he could almost see images of the scenes Ned was telling him about in the smoke.

"But I get ahead of myself again," Ned said with a laugh. "Of these things I shall come to. It is my early days that concern us here, is it not?"

And before Fred could respond, he went on: "I went into the Chestnut Street Theater one day and saw the great Ellen Terry performing the part of Rosalind in Shakespeare's *As You Like It*. She was beautiful, Fred. Quite lovely. Then over the following week I saw her as Viola in *Twelfth Night* and Beatrice in *Much Ado About Nothing*. And though I had never heard of Shakespeare before, I was entranced, captivated by his way with words. I watched as the audience were enchanted by the actors and the plays and I determined then that one day I would be a wordsmith like Shakespeare."

He blew out a smoke ring and laughed. "Well, I may not have achieved the level of Shakespeare, but I think I can fairly claim to have made my mark on American Literature."

"You are the equal of any of them, Colonel. Mark Twain, James Fennimore Cooper, Henry Wadsworth Longfellow and Nathaniel Hawthorne, you can hold your head up among them all."

Ned sat up at mention of their names, for Fred had touched a raw spot. As a young writer with a few articles under his belt he had presented his visiting card to several literary lions, only to have been snubbed by some and ignored by others. Such memories he was quick to expunge swiftly whenever they found their way into his conscious thoughts.

He grinned. "Oh, they may not think I am their equal, Fred, but the common man, the worker, the shop assistant and all of the folk who do the work that makes America great, they may just sit back with a Ned Buntline novel or one of my magazines and gain some solace and entertainment from my words."

"And aspiring authors like me, Colonel. I have made it my aim to put you up there where you belong, with the literary giants of our great nation."

"Ha! You are a good fellow, Fred. It would not be for me to claim such heights. Yet I daresay that I have sold far more books and overall penned more words than all of them put together."

He suddenly jumped up, forgetting his gouty foot for a moment until a stab of pain brought a curse from his lips.

"My pardon for my language, Fred. Such nautical words often creep out unbidden in unguarded moments, like that. All a legacy of my days at sea."

"I hoped you would come to that, Colonel," said Fred enthusiastically.

"After lunch, Fred. I suggest that you go and prepare yourself and ask my dear wife if she will be serving fresh lemonade at luncheon. As a temperance advocate I cannot get enough of it."

Fred left him puffing contentedly on his pipe.

Two minutes later Ned had crossed the room and quietly turned the key in the lock. Then he crept over to the suit of armor and pulled up the visor of the helmet. He reached inside until his arm was inside the chest and from it he drew out a flask of Old Abner's moonshine. He licked his lips, uncorked it and then supped liberally with relish.

Temperance be damned for today, he thought. Having a young disciple hanging on my every word is a thirst-making business. You have deserved this Ned. Sup, my friend.

And that is exactly what he did, savoring the pleasant glow as the hot liquor hit his stomach.

Chapter 3

A LIFE ON THE OCEAN WAVE

During lunch Ned enthused about Anna's choice of menu, which was unusual and had clearly been determined by her food cravings and aversions, both consequences of her childbearing condition.

Fred Pond sat enjoying the home-made lemonade and the strange mélange of dishes, which Santiago, their Mexican cook had managed to prepare in a skillful manner, despite his reservations about mixing fish with coconut, pigeon with oranges, and garlic with pickles, followed by apple pie and horseradish relish.

The young writer was continually amazed at the ease with which Ned could keep up a continual conversation, more often a monologue than dialogue, flitting from subject to subject with barely a pause or an obvious link betwixt them. He talked about his books, the different types of fly for fishing and the reasons for choosing them, the skills in tracking that he had been taught by the Pawnee, the reasons for using living wood when water-divining and the best ways of breaking a horse in.

Anna interjected every now and then when she

thought he was getting too verbose or seemed in danger of boring Fred, but each time Fred protested politely and urged Ned onwards.

"I think that you may have had too much of that lemonade, Edward. You know how the bubbles go to your head," she said with mock reproval.

Ned laughed. "Why Hazel Eyes, you would think that I was drinking the demon drink, instead of this divine libation of yours."

With which he launched into a diatribe about the health benefits of temperance and the need to reduce the supply of strong liquor to those who could not cope with it.

"Here, here, Colonel," said Fred, raising his glass and laughing. "This is the finest lemonade I ever tasted and I concur, the bubbles seem to go right to one's head."

"What you need is a siesta, Fred," Ned said. "A sleep after your lunch."

Anna smiled and sipped her lemonade. "Edward often has one and sleeps like a baby for an hour or two. Then he might work solidly for twelve hours without eating another thing. Why I have sometimes left him lying on his front upon the floor, writing away with a quill and paper and found him still writing next morning when I have risen."

"It is the way of the writer, my Angel," Ned explained. "I learned to write in that position when I was a sailor. As for the siesta, it clears the mind and fires the furnaces of the imagination. It is in such a way that I can in a few days complete three dime novels or a six-hundred-page novel or even a serial of twenty or so episodes. I learned about the siesta from some sailors when I was sailing the Spanish Main. From Genoa in Italy they were from and they extoled the virtues of the siesta, although when sailing they had no opportunity to have one. Ah, but on shore leave, why hardly a one of them could be found awake between two o'clock and four."

He winked at Fred. "Of course, that may in part have been because they drank gallons of beer and rum all night."

He wiped his mouth with his serviette and then clapped his hands.

"And with your leave, my Hazel Eyes, and by yours good Fred Pond, I shall leave you as I climb the stairs to my chamber, and there as Shakespeare's Hamlet would say, 'to sleep, perchance to dream.' I will see you all anon."

And standing to execute a bow, he left.

Within twenty seconds of his head hitting the pillow Ned fell into a deep sleep all the while emitting a snore that would do justice to a grizzly bear. His body was well accustomed to sleep off the half quart of moonshine that he had consumed before lunch. He knew that upon waking his gout would play him up a tad, but he accepted it as the penalty for railing against alcohol while being a confirmed imbiber. Actual guilt was essentially foreign emotion to Ned Buntline.

At Anna's urging, Fred Pond had followed suit and retired to his room for a siesta. There he found his mind was buzzing with ideas and questions, so that it took him some time to fall into a doze. Yet when he woke he knew what questions he wanted to ask the great man.

The opportunity to ask came as they played pool and smoked cigars in Ned's games room later that afternoon.

"I am intrigued how you became so knowledgeable about the sea, Colonel. Your novels about the West, hunting and adventuring I can understand, but I would not have placed you as a seaman."

Ned was eyeing up a tricky shot. He leaned over the green beige, his cigar clamped between his lips in the corner of his mouth while he placed his hand in an open bridge position so that he could use the V between thumb and index finger to rest the cue. He lined it up and after his habitual three practice moves made the shot.

He grunted with satisfaction as the targeted ball dropped into the pocket and he then proceeded to clear up the rest of the balls on the table.

"You are not alone there, Fred. A lot of people over the years have not considered that I fitted their image of a sailor. In the same way I have not conformed to their idea of what a writer, soldier, politician, bounty hunter or playwright should look like, yet I have been all of those things and many more besides."

He stubbed his cigar out on the side of a large copper spittoon that had once graced Nuttall and Mann's Saloon in Deadwood and dropped the butt inside. He had already told Fred that it used to be placed to the side of the poker table that Wild Bill Hickok habitually used until the afternoon he drew eights and aces in black just moments before a low down squirt called Jack McCall shot him in the back of the head. He promised him other tales of Hickok later on.

"As I told you this morning, whenever I could get away from the rigorous schooling in law that my father was giving me I roamed Philadelphia the same way I previously roamed the countryside at Dyberry Creek. The theaters were an obvious attraction to me, but so too were the Front Street docks. I was a bit of a wharf rat, mooching around, opportunistically sneaking on board clippers to smell the oranges and spices brought over from India, the molasses from the West Indies and the crates of tea from China. I loved the jostling of the old sea dogs with their waddling gaits from years walking on moving decks, the cries of the teamsters bringing cargo or unloading it, and the noise of wagon wheels and horses clattering over the cobbles. I was intrigued by the merchants and ship owners in their tall beaver hats with their fat wallets, their huge cigars and bags of gold. Above all I loved the smell of it all, the sound of the seagulls circling overhead and the sheer exoticism of the places the boats had visited. In my mind I made up all sorts of stories of pirates and privateers."

He circled the table scooping the balls from the pockets and then racked them up again.

"I got to know a lot of the men who worked there and they got to know me, the red-headed kid that wouldn't stay away. Some even gave me small nips of grog or rum in exchange for an errand to buy a twist of tobacco or a newspaper."

He stared wistfully ahead, reliving the life on the docks, smelling the oil, the tar and the brine.

"There was all this excitement, Fred, but whenever I got home my father wanted me to plough my way through law books. "The Law, that is the place for you, Edward. One day we shall be lawyers together," he would say. You see, he was convinced that I was ideally suited to the legal profession. The trouble was that my mind craved something more interesting and my mind wandered. Whenever it did, I received a thump on the head with one of those great, thick law books."

He rubbed the back of his head as if recollecting the chastisements, then he tapped a shelf with his cue, drawing Fred's attention for the first time to a plaster bust of a man. Fred noticed that the scalp was covered in small colored squares and circles, each with writing on them.

"That is a phrenological bust, Fred. Have you seen one before?"

"I have seen them advertised in magazines, Colonel. But I have never seen one in real life."

"Phrenology is a remarkably accurate science of the mind that I have been interested in since I was a youngster. In fact, ever since my father took me to see Doctor Johann Spurzheim in Boston, Massachusetts."

"That was some journey, Colonel."

"It was indeed, Fred. We seemed to be on the railroad forever, at least to my youthful mind. Yet my father was determined that I should be seen by the most renowned specialist in America. You see, Doctor Spurzheim was a physician and an anatomist, who had studied phrenology under its founder, Doctor Franz Joseph Gall in Paris, France. He was on a world lecture tour and was giving daily lectures at Harvard University. In order to spread the word about the science of phrenology he was giving consultations at a clinic at Massachusetts General Hospital."

"Did your father think you were ill?"

Ned laughed. "He thought I wasn't right in my head, that is for sure. He wanted advice that I really was suited to follow him into the law. Anyway, Doctor Johann Spurzheim was an interesting fellow. I can see him now. He was tall with an angular, unsmiling face. He had receding hair, which he tried to conceal with brilliantine, sculpting his scant wisps of hair into a sort of widow's peak. He had long pork chop whiskers, a ramrod straight back and a crisp continental accent. When we came in he stood up, clicked his heels and gave us the shortest of bows, rather than shake hands. 'My hands, they are delicate instruments,' he said. 'I can feel the finest nuance on the skull, so that it is like I am caressing the brain of my patient, *ja*. Now this is the boy, Edward you said his name was in your letter.' Then he examined my head."

Ned's expression changed as he took on the character of Dr. Spurzheim. He moved his hands, mimicking the examination of his own skull. " '*Ja*, it is clear to me. He has a very large head, this boy.' "

Ned's posture changed as did his voice as he assumed his father's manner and character. " 'Yes. He is a conceited boy.' "

" '*Ja*! Never have I felt a boy's head with so many lumps. He has potential in so many areas.' "

Ned guffawed. "I said that it was all due to my father. The phrenologist nodded and said it was good to have respect for one's parents. What I had really meant, though, was that my lumps were due to my father repeatedly striking me about the head with his blasted law books."

Fred chortled at the thought, which encouraged Ned to be even more theatrical in his depiction of the examination of his skull by the German phrenologist.

" 'Ach! He has enormous potential in the faculties of vivativeness, continuity, approbativeness and conscientiousness.' "

Ned waved his hand, becoming his father's character again. " 'No, that can't be right. Not the last one. He is anything but conscientious.' "

Then Ned as Spurzheim, scowled. " 'Nein! You are wrong. It is written here in the boy's skull. He is conscientious in the subjects he likes.' "

His father's character nodded. " 'Ah, that must mean he is stubborn. In that case, I concur.' "

Ned, as the Spurzheim character continued. " 'He has incredible imagination and he is adventurous. He has a capacity for philoprogenitiveness and for amativeness.' "

The great writer winked at Fred Pond and whispered as an aside, "I looked all of those terms up later, Fred. They have been emblazoned on my memory ever since."

Then resuming his father's role, his expression changed to one of puzzlement. " 'I am not familiar with these terms.' "

Instantly, changing role again, as Spurzheim, Ned lowered his voice. " 'He will be popular with the ladies.' "

Ned again laughed. "My father didn't like that,

so he got to the rub. 'In summary, Doctor, can you tell me whether this boy will be suited to the legal profession?' He sat drumming his fingers on the arms of the chair, a habit of his when his patience was wearing thin."

Once more the German phrenologist appeared. " 'Why yes. He will be perfect. He has a capacity for cunning. He has a facility with language. He does not mind telling untruths. He would make a perfect lawyer.' "

Picking up his pipe, Ned struck a light and puffed it contentedly. "Of course, that was precisely what my father wanted to hear. The fact that the doctor hadn't actually communicated a word with me, just examined my head, didn't matter to my parent. So, we went home and over the next few months he continued to tutor me in the law."

"And you did so happily?"

"Not happily, Fred, but it was the easiest way of keeping the peace. Whenever I could I slipped off to the theater or to the docks. Then as time went by I grew more restless, for I knew it just wasn't what I was interested in. Then one day I had enough. I rebelled and threw his copy of *Blackstone's Commentaries* into the grate. I laughed as it caught fire, page after page. My father came in and was not amused one whit. He struck me across the face and knocked me flying."

Ned flung himself backwards onto the settee behind him, automatically reliving the part.

"Up I sprang," he said, nimbly righting himself and ignoring the pain in his gouty foot. "I stared at him but said nary a word. Instead, I turned and ran out the door. I did not stop until I reached the Front Street dock. Then on and on I went until I reached the Arch. A schooner had just cast off and so I ran and bounded aboard."

He reached for his oilskin tobacco pouch and began charging his corncob pipe.

"That was it, Fred. At the age of eleven I had run away to sea aboard the *Mary Cairn*, a fruit schooner bound for the West Indies, although I didn't know that at the time."

Fred Pond stared in amazement. "Just like that? On the spur of the moment?"

"It is how I have led a large part of my life, Fred. By my wits and the speed of my actions. Virtually every one of those five hundred dime novels you looked at in my study has some basis in fact. My life's adventures are woven into those pages."

"But did the ship's captain not think to turn about and find your family?"

"The captain didn't know about me straight away, Fred. By the time we entered Delaware Bay the boat was on its way to the West Indies and every hour was accountable. Time is money, you see, and as the sea and the winds can be capricious, no captain is going to turn his ship around for an orphan."

"But you weren't an orphan, Colonel. You had a family; a mother, father and sister at home."

"I felt bad about leaving mother and sister, but I vowed that I would have nothing more to do with my father. I had struck out on my own. Fortunately, when the ship's mate finally collared me and hauled me before old Captain Fred Skinner, I had already shown my adroitness at climbing rigging. I had evaded twenty sailors by springing, climbing and swinging."

He grinned as he struck fire to his pipe. "The captain needed a cabin boy and I was there, able and willing. They asked my name and I told them it was Edward. Captain Skinner shook his head and told me that wouldn't do. He wouldn't have a landlubber name like that on his ship. Instead I was to be Ned. And since I said I had no second name, because I didn't want there to be any way that I could be sent home to my father when we returned to port, he gave me a second name."

"What did he call you, Colonel?"

"He said I reminded him of the twists of a buntline hitch. In case you didn't know it, a buntline is the line used to handle the square sails on a clipper. The buntline hitch is the sailor's knot used to secure it. So, Ned Buntline I was called and for good or ill, Ned Buntline I have been all of my writing life."

Fred chuckled as he scribbled some notes. "A buntline! Brilliant! Did you enjoy that first nautical adventure, Colonel?"

Ned tamped down the smoldering tobacco with his thumb. "It was not an easy trip, Fred. For eight days we sailed before the breeze and then a storm hit us, and I truly thought that we were going to be capsized. I was petrified but thrilled at the same time. I vowed that if I survived, I would one day write an adventure about it. Yet suffice to say that we did survive and that after some days we found our way to Havana in Cuba. There, Captain Skinner took me with him to stay at his lady love's home."

He grinned. " 'Tis true, Fred. A sailor really does have a girl in every port. At least Captain Skinner did. And I have to say, that Havana was the first port that I lost my heart in. To the captain's lady love's daughter, actually. In fact, I lost more than my heart, for in her arms I became a man."

Fred Pond blushed, but said nothing.

"Once the ship was reloaded we left Havana and sailed back. On the way, for it was a calm sailing, I learned from the sailors how to carve seashells or tiny mermaids from wood, how to put a miniature ship in a bottle and how to tie every type of knot needed aboard a ship. I loved every minute of it."

He grimaced and sucked air through his teeth.

"But my father was waiting on the wharf when we docked in Philadelphia. He greeted me stiffly."

Ned suddenly adopted the posture of a martinet. " 'So sir, you have returned?' he said to me. 'I suppose you are sick of the sea and are willing to ask my forgiveness; and if I permit you to come home, to do as I wish, not as you will, eh?' "

Then he stood with his hands behind his back, the years dropping from his face as he shook his head. "No sir, I ask no home of you, for I have found a dearer home upon the sea. It has been my privilege to meet friends, all honest men and true, who shared that oaken home, that ship with me. Not one of them would strike me as you struck me."

Ned shook his head. "That upset my father, which I was pleased about, for I have to admit that I had been planning and preparing for our meeting for many days."

Again he straightened to take on the role of his father. " 'Is this your choice, degenerate boy! A life of hardship and peril, shared with such associates! Is this the life which you choose instead of the luxury and ease you would have, simply through studying the law under my tutelage?' "

Fred stared transfixed. "You stood up to your father like that when you were just a boy of eleven years?"

Ned winked at the younger writer. "I was

no longer a boy, Fred, as I just told you. Our conversation went on for some time, with my father cajoling and sometimes threatening me, all to no avail. I told him that 'Resurgam' is my motto—independence my character! So I bade him farewell. He stared at me with fury, but at last, he said he disowned me before turning around and stomping off along the wharf."

He stopped to relight his pipe.

"All of this had been watched by Captain Skinner. He noted the tears in my eyes and told me to cheer up, for he would be a father to me. A shrewd fellow he was. He told me not to be down-hearted, for grief was like an anchor in the hold. It could weigh the ship down without being of any use. I took him at his word and when the ship was loaded again we set sail with a cargo of flour for Rio de Janeiro."

"What sights I saw upon the sea, Fred. Whales, dolphins, seals and even mermaids, I swear. I saw coral reefs, giant squids and octopi. And what adventures as we sailed the Spanish Main. We saw slaver ships and kept a wide berth of them and of those ships that looked suspiciously like pirates."

"Did you ever fight any pirates?"

"Only a few times," Ned replied instantly with the nonchalance that Fred had already noted characterized those anecdotes which he told so humbly. "You see, Captain Skinner had a sense of humor. Sometimes we would catch sight of a merchantman and would purposefully follow it, giving the impression that we ourselves might be pirates. We did that four times, letting the ship get away on three occasions, but on the other keeping up the pretense until the ship finally gave up its flight and surrendered. Then the captain and crew informed them of the joke and, rather than a fight ensuing, so overcome were they by relief that we were given a cask of brandy and a supply of tobacco."

He stared at the blue smoke rings that he sent ceilingwards. "It was then that I first developed my passion for a good pipe and a cigar."

Fred nodded, feeling slightly sick from the haze of smoke that hung in the air.

Ned went on: "I stayed with Captain Skinner for three years until I felt it was time to stretch my wings and cast out on my own. I had learned much, but I wanted to forge out a career, so I enlisted in the navy as an apprentice, which as you may know, is the lowest of the low. Well, one winter's day I was given a punishment for talking back to an officer. I'm afraid it was a weakness of mine, especially when I considered the officer to be in the wrong or just plain dumb. My punishment on this occasion was to take a boat to Staten Island and return with a load of sand. So, there I was, the coxswain of a boat heading up the East River in a thick fog as darkness was falling, when we were run over by a Fulton ferry-boat. The men were thrown overboard into the icy water, while the ferry-boat careened away, totally unaware that they had hit us."

Fred made notes. "That must have been terrifying, Colonel."

"It was. We were foundering, Fred, but I managed to haul all of the men back onto the stricken vessel. Then I ordered them to dump the sand to help keep us afloat and I managed to keep all of their spirits up. Luck was with us and a sloop, the *Helen Morley* picked us all up. Of course, when we landed on the south wharf the men wanted to revive their spirits with grog, but I stopped them and ordered them to march to the navy yard. Then I fainted away, because I had broken my arm and at least two ribs.

"Two weeks I spent in the sick bay, half delirious with fever. When I came around I discovered that my little exploit had not gone unnoticed. The crew had been vocal to the officers and told them of how I had saved their lives. A recommendation had gone to the president that I was officer material, the result being that on February 10, 1838, Martin Van Buren himself signed my midshipman's papers."

Ned tapped out his pipe and immediately recharged it. He struck light and soon had it belching fumes again.

"On a journey south, the other midshipmen were jealous of my elevation and refused to mess with me, because they thought I was not worthy. I reacted to such slights as I always have, by challenging them. Four of them I gave a thrashing in boxing bouts, two others I marked for life, and received this scar on my cheek, and another on my back from knife wounds. Another two I challenged to duels.

"The captain heard of this and knew of my marksmanship. In order to dissuade the other middys from making a fatal mistake, he had a bottle of brandy hung on the yardarm and had me shoot it. I had no trouble, of course. My first shot smashed it and the second cut the string that had held it."

Fred clapped his hands. "Bravo, Colonel."

Ned shook his hands dismissively. "It was nothing, but the captain undoubtedly saved their hides, for although I would have striven to merely wound them, yet a duel is a duel and if one's life is dependent upon it, the wounds I would have inflicted could have proven mortal, for gunshot wounds often fester and cause death."

"Did they hold malice against you, Colonel?"

"On the contrary, Fred. They became my staunch comrades later during the Seminole War. But before I tell you, why don't you go and get us some more of my wife's excellent lemonade."

As soon as Fred Pond had gone off to fetch the

lemonade Ned was on his feet. He pulled back the cue rack and opened the hidden recess where he kept one of his flagons of moonshine.

Talking is thirsty work, Ned, he mused to himself. So saying, he raised the flagon in a toast to the small Old Glory flag that hung above the pool table. Then he quenched his thirst, reveling in the memories that came flooding into his mind.

NOTEBOOK 4
Property of Fred E. Pond
Private & Confidential

JOTTINGS ON THE LIFE OF NED BUNTLINE
April 1881

Note 16
I suspect that either Colonel Judson is not so devoted to the temperance cause as he professes, or he reacts very jovially to lemonade.

Chapter 4

THE SEMINOLE WAR

Fred was surprised to find that Ned had completely lost his desire for lemonade when he returned with a fresh pitcher and two glasses.

"Fresh air, that is what we need rather than more libations for the throat. Let us instead put on coats and venture forth to Stamford. We shall ride, if you would get Solomon to saddle up two steeds for us to sally forth."

Somewhat confused, yet eager to see the town, Fred did as suggested and met Ned half an hour later at the stables. Ned came limping out, leaning on his stick. As he mounted his horse Fred saw that he had a Navy Colt holstered at his side and was about to remark on it when Ned suddenly cried out in pain as his foot found the stirrup.

"Is this a good idea, Colonel? With your gout, I mean. Would not a buggy have been a more suitable means of travel?"

"Pah! A buggy, did you say? I will take one when escorting Hazel Eyes to church on a Sunday, but on land the only suitable conveyance for a man is a good horse."

As they rode, Ned picked up on his tales of the

navy. "Although I was little more than a lad, a midshipman, yet I was given authority because the officers thought I merited it and could handle it. My guiding principle was 'never order anyone to do something I wouldn't be prepared to do myself.' That was why the men, seasoned sailors were prepared to follow my lead, whether it be to head for shore or sail to hell."

He grinned at Fred. "Once, when I was in command of a gunboat, as the captain was ill with yellow jaundice, in heavy mist we came across a British Man O'War. For a jape and a dare I swam out to it, boarded it clandestinely like Captain Dan Maltravers, the hero of three dime novels I would write years later, shinnied up the main mast and stole their Union Jack. The crew could scarce believe it when I swam back to our boat with the trophy."

" 'Wring it out and stuff it in the cannon,' I commanded. 'We'll give them a broadside that they won't forget. It will teach them never to let some pirate steal their colors.' "

Fred stared in amazement. "You actually fired on a British Man O'War?"

"We did, then we sailed off into the fog before they knew anything. I heard later that they found their flag floating on the water with a hole in the middle. Apparently, the captain had it hoisted again, and they let it be known that it had taken a direct hit during an engagement with buccaneers.

I did them a favor, you see, for it gave them a reputation."

"I get the impression that you are not enamored of the British, are you, Colonel?"

Ned snorted. "Oh, I have personally known a few and they have been fine fellows for the most part." He stroked his mustache and smiled as if recollecting encounters and past relationships. "And I have known several English and Scottish ladies. I really did get on well with them. But as a nation, well you have only to look at the history of our great country, Fred. The British exploited us, which is why we fought a war and declared our independence. My father's book, *A Biography of the Signers of the Declaration of Independence*, says it all. I didn't agree with a lot of the things he spouted about, but he was right there. No, Fred, America is for Americans and I am against immigration in general."

Fred made another mental note to explore the colonel's views in greater detail in the days ahead. "Did you enjoy your naval days, Colonel?"

"I did indeed. I loved the navy, Fred. It enabled me to see much of the world. By the time I was eighteen I had seen New York, New Orleans, Charleston, the Caribbean and ports all the way down to Tierra del Fuego. I saw adventure and I saw action, what more could a young man want?"

He shook his head. "But the thing about

being in the navy was the discipline. You had to obey orders, whether or not you agreed with them. That went for me as a mere midshipman, just the same as it did for the captain, or even the admiral of the fleet. For example, I cannot say that I agreed with Old Hickory, President Andrew Jackson's policy of Indian Removal to land west of the Mississippi. As you know, the army sent countless troops into Florida to defeat the Seminole after the Dade Massacre. Osceola, the great chief was captured and died in prison and gradually the fight went out of the remaining Seminole who were rounded up and sent west. All except his nephew Shadow Cloud."

"I had not heard of him, Colonel."

"Not many had, but I would live to rue his existence, just as I suspect he rued mine. The year was 1840 and I was by that time Acting Lieutenant of US Schooner *Otego*, part of McLaughlin's Mosquito Fleet. We were tasked with subduing and detaining any Indian parties on shore.

"We were dispatched to the Everglades and sent to land. Our mission was to march inland until we intersected the Miami River, then follow it downstream to Fort Dallas on Biscayne Bay. I as Acting Lieutenant had Walter Gibson, one of the midshipmen I had bested in a knife fight, under my command as well as half a dozen young apprentices and two other midshipmen."

"And you were just what, sixteen years old?" Fred asked in admiration.

Ned nodded. "But with some years of experience and my own independent character and some proven mettle in conflict. It was slow going and I was aware that Walter Gibson, who one day would become Admiral Gibson, was getting restless. I deemed it worth allowing him to assume command, since it would show him that I trusted his ability and it would show those under us that I could delegate and also that he could rise to the occasion. Apart from that, I was eager to go hunting. I knew that I could allow myself some time, for I would easily be able to track and overtake the detail.

"It was not long before I came across the spoor of a cougar and I started to track it. My old Pawnee warrior would have loved the chase as I stalked it to the side of a lagoon and began to creep up on it, intent on a clean kill. That was my mistake, Fred, because I the stalker had unbeknownst to me suddenly became the stalked. The creature pounced from behind me. Had I not had lightning fast reflexes and pitched sideward, it would have done for me then and there. As it was, it slashed my back as it passed, and I dropped my weapon. It turned as soon as it landed and leaped straight at me, its claws out and its mouth gaping, ready to fix on my throat.

"But I had instinctively pulled out my long

dagger and I skewered it through the throat mere inches before its jaws would have clamped and torn into the flesh of my own neck. I put it out of its agony, of course, like any good hunter. I will show you the slash wounds it gave me later."

"It must have hurt terribly, Colonel?"

"It did, but when you have had as many wounds as I have—indeed, as many as I had acquired, even then—well, you just keep going. The problem was more the amount of blood that I would lose, so I made myself a makeshift poultice of moss and spider webs to stanch the bleeding. It is an old Indian remedy, Fred. You would do well to remember it."

Stamford was looming ahead of them and Ned stopped his mount and reached into his pockets for his corncob pipe and tobacco pouch. Soon he had the pipe charged and had struck a light to it.

"I carried the cougar over my shoulders and soon calculated the terrain that I needed to cover to catch up on my fellows. By this time the sun was high overhead and I estimated that Walter would be allowing them to break their march for refreshments soon. Imagine my horror when I came across broken shrubbery and trampled ground, dotted here and there with bloodstains.

"A quick examination allowed me to build up a tableau of what had happened. The moccasined footprints and the holes in trees where arrowheads had been pulled out made it all too clear.

My men had been attacked and taken by the Seminole."

Fred Pond jotted down the details of the Everglades exploit on his notebook that he had affixed to the back of his saddle horn.

"I reluctantly left my prized cougar and devoted my tracking skills to the task in hand," Ned went on. "I followed, knowing full well that the Seminole party numbered two more than the nine who had been under my command. I could make no plan until I knew precisely what the state of my men was and what the Seminole party had in store for them.

"I caught up to them, the last part of the journey being made sidewinder fashion on my belly. Fortunately, my facility with Indian languages allowed me to ascertain exactly what was what. My men were all tied to trees, two to a tree and were being guarded by two Seminole Indians. Their fellows had gone off, presumably to report the capture of Americans to their chief, Shadow Cloud. They intended ransoming them, but if anyone attempted to rescue them, they were to be quickly dispatched by the knife."

Fred stared in horror. "You must have agonized as to what action to take."

Ned shook his head. "I had no choice. I had to rescue them as soon as an opportunity presented itself. It came when the younger of the two announced that he was going into the woods to catch some food. I waited for some time after he had gone, then rushed into the clearing, startling my comrades, who were all bound and gagged and who, to a man, looked petrified.

"The remaining Seminole guard was quick for a big fellow, but not quick enough. I caught him in the chest with a flying kick that sent him hurtling back to crash against a tree. But he recovered in an instant and whipped out a tomahawk, which he threw straight at me. I ducked, and it embedded in the tree just inches above Walter Gibson's head.

"That made me mad and I dashed forward, gave him a swift one-two, then struck him with an uppercut that lifted him off his feet, rattled his jaw and knocked out two teeth before he was deposited on his back, out cold.

"I had to work fast and bound and gagged him before he could recover and send a signal to his fellows, who could be close at hand, for all I knew. I then approached Walter, knife in hand to cut his bonds.

"As I came close I saw the look of alarm in his eyes and immediately threw myself sideways, just in time to hear the whoosh as an arrow flew towards me. Then I felt excruciating pain in my left arm and I was spun around with the force of it. I looked down to see the arrow embedded in my upper arm, blood spurting freely from the wound.

"Even then I saw the other Seminole guard bringing another arrow up to fire again. I rolled over, coming to my feet in an instant, ignoring the pain and the blood loss and threw my knife straight at my would-be killer. My aim was true and it hit the bow, as I intended, smashing it in two in his hands. And then I was running and launched myself on him, pummeling him unconscious with my good fist, with the fury of my situation. Yet I stopped short of killing him, for that was not my intention. Instead, I climbed to my feet and cut Walter and my comrades free before I slumped to the ground."

Fred stared aghast. "All that blood you had lost, and you could still do that? That is amazing, Colonel."

In answer, despite the cold, Ned stripped off his coat and pulled up his buckskins to reveal his back, which was a veritable mass of old scars.

"The cougar's slashes as well as assorted wounds from Indian fighting, knife brawls and a couple of Civil War wounds from Confederate bullets," he announced. And then he exposed his arm and the large white scar upon his biceps. "Behold the arrow wound."

Fred shook his head in amazement as Ned pulled his buckskins back down and drew his coat about him again. "Your body looks like a patchwork quilt of wounds and scars, Colonel."

Ned nodded and gave a short laugh. "Arrow

wounds are far more dangerous than bullet wounds, Fred. They are more likely to fester, so you have to be careful how you treat them. As soon as he was free Walter Gibson was keen to pluck that arrow out of my arm, but I wouldn't let him."

"Why not, Colonel?"

"Because of the way that arrows are made, with the head attached to the shaft by animal sinews. If you try to pull them out, the shaft will come away and leave the arrowhead. I told Walter that, and so, with his help I shoved it all the way through the arm and out the other side. Then I let him snap it off and pull the shaft back through. As soon as he did it I knew that I could afford to let myself go and I felt myself passing out.

" 'It's over to you, now, Walter. Get us all back to Fort Dallas and out of the reach of Shadow Cloud,' I told him."

"And did he?"

"He did and we both received medals for our action. As I said earlier, he went on to eventually become an admiral and I . . . well, I went on to more modest things. But we left the two Indians tied up to trees. Some weeks later we heard from a scout that Shadow Cloud had sent me, as the American fighter who bested his two braves, a present. It was the tomahawk that the larger of the two had thrown at me, and which almost took Walter Gibson's head off. The Indian who delivered the present said that the great chief hoped to meet me one day—so that he could have the honor in combat of burying the tomahawk in my skull."

Fred stared with open mouth for a moment. "I'd have been terrified at such a thing. To think that someone hated me so much, that they gave me the very weapon they meant to kill me with one day."

Ned gave a rueful smile then his characteristic short laugh. Fred was getting used to it and deduced that it meant that Ned scoffed at danger.

"I took that as a compliment, Fred. He meant it as an honor, I think, from one warrior to another. I have had many men say that they'd like to do similar or worse things to me, but that's the one that makes the hairs on the back of my neck stand up with pride."

Fred shook his head in wonder. Truly, he believed that Colonel Edward Judson spat in the face of danger.

"Anyway, by the end of the Seminole War I had been promoted to lieutenant and had served with valor and distinction under Jessup, Gaines, Armistead and Worth. A glittering career lay ahead of me, General Walker Armistead told me, and he said that it would not be long before I had a ship under my own command. Yet I was restless for land. I still had dreams of living the life of Daniel Boone, so I resigned from the service and gained employment with the Northwest Fur Company. I went up the Yellowstone River and hunted elk in the Rockies, buffalo on the plains and had more than my fair share of encounters with grizzly bears."

"Like the one back at the Eagle's Nest."

"Just so, although that one I shot on a later trip, when I, Texas Jack Omohundro and Buffalo Bill Cody were leading a hunting party organized for the Grand Duke Alexei Alexandrovich of Russia. We were riding with three generals, General Philip Sheridan, General Edward Ord and General George Armstrong Custer. It was something of a circus rather than a proper hunt and Bill Cody and I had previously arranged with Spotted Tail, chief of the Brulé Lakota to gather six hundred Sioux to meet the 'great chief from across the water.' They put on a great exhibition of horsemanship, lance throwing and bow-shooting. Suffice to say that the Grand Duke was thrilled, although he was a lousy shot himself and had to have animals herded right up in front of him to have a chance of hitting one."

Ned chuckled. "I wrote all about it in *The Knickerbocker Magazine*, of course, and used it later as the basis for three dime novels. The grizzly I met afterwards when I was making my own way back and soaking up the scenery to write a book on hunting. I dispatched him when he thought it a good idea to disturb me when I was building a campfire to make coffee."

"And you hauled the body back by yourself?"

"I had a pack mule with me, so I made it to a railhead and had it sent to my taxidermist back East. But I have got ahead of myself again, Fred. I was telling you about my days in 1843, when I worked for the Northwest Fur Company. After a few months, when I became their most successful hunter ever I got itchy feet again. When I stopped off at Eddyville in Kentucky I heard that three bad men had robbed a bank and murdered a bank teller in Gallatin. A posse hadn't been able to catch them, but word was they were holed up in the woods. That peeved me, Fred, because I can't abide bank robbing and it made my blood boil to hear that they had killed a man who was just doing his job. I decided there and then to put my tracking skills to further good use."

"You went after them alone?"

"I did. It didn't take me long to pick up their trail and I fired a warning shot over their heads. One of them rode off, but the other two took to the brush and aimed to shoot it out with me. I won't bore you with the details, but I easily outmanoeuvred them, nicking both with well-aimed shots so that they surrendered. I tied them to trees, then went in hot pursuit of the third one. Unfortunately, he had too big a start on me and I gave up the chase.

"The two outlaws that I had tied up were both bleeding from the nicks I had inflicted upon them and cursed me most foully. That I disliked and told them so in no uncertain terms as I tended to their wounds. Suitably chastised when I reminded them that the law would deal harshly with murderers, they both claimed that the other, a fellow by the name of Sutton, had fired the fatal shot and that they had been scared of him themselves."

"But you got them back on your own?"

"Uh huh. I hog-tied them and laid them over their own horses and then took them back to Eddyville. There I lashed them back to back and took them by steamer to Gallatin, where the sheriff took them off my hands. I collected six hundred dollars reward for them and immediately gave it to the bank teller's parents." He shook his head. "It was scant recompense for their son's life, but what else could I do?"

Fred stored the anecdote up and planned to write it out when they arrived at Hamilton House. "It was a noble act, Colonel."

Ned waved a hand dismissively and put on his most self-deprecating expression. "Anyone would have done it."

He knew, of course, that wasn't true.

Chapter 5

DISCRETION

They hitched their horses outside the five storied Hamilton House Hotel and prepared to mount the stoop when Jimmy Carson the hotel clerk came rushing out. He was a gaunt young man of around thirty, with sparse, receding hair that he clearly tried to disguise by combing over from one side.

"Colonel Judson, sir. I thought I had better warn you there might be danger in there for you, sir. I didn't want you to get ambushed."

"A . . . Ambushed?" Fred repeated, apprehensively.

Ned stiffened and drew himself erect to his full five foot six inches. He mounted the stoop and Fred followed with a measure of caution.

"I appreciate your concern, Jimmy," said Ned. "How many of them are there and what is their beef?"

"There are three of them, Colonel. Two men and a woman. The woman is a lady, dressed in black, with a veil. As for the men, well they look—capable."

Ned's hand tightened on the head of his stick. "Hmm. A widow, do you mean?"

Fred darted a glance at the colonel and saw a jaw muscle twitch. He was not sure whether it was a look of worry on the writer's face. He turned and addressed the hotel clerk. "What do you mean, they look capable, sir? Capable of what?"

Jimmy peered at Fred and a hint of amusement played across his lips. "Capable of holding their own in a fight, sir."

Ned tapped his stick on the stoop. "A widow?" he repeated. "And she wants to see me?" he asked.

"I didn't say she was a widow, Colonel Judson, sir. You did. I said she was wearing black and had a veil. She's drunk a lot of coffee and more whiskey than I've ever seen a lady drink." He did an impromptu imitation of the said lady lifting the bottom of her veil and drinking a glass of whiskey. "She's done a lot of talking, too, Colonel. In fact, I heard that she and the two men had been in several of the establishments in town asking questions. Then when they came here she's talked to just about every one of the hotel guests and everyone else who's eaten in the restaurant or stopped for a drink in the bar."

Ned eyed him askance. "Talked about what, Jimmy? Out with it."

Jimmy coughed to clear his throat and then leaned toward them. "She's been talking about you, Colonel. I hear that she's spread it all round town that you are a lying, cheating snake. She says she is going to expose you, Colonel."

Fred noticed Ned's face grow alabaster white. He saw his prominent Adam's apple bob up and down as if he had sudden difficulty swallowing.

"She may be planning to visit the Eagle's Nest, Colonel," Jimmy went on. "She has been talking to guests in the lobby and asking if they know how she might get there."

"Did . . . did you say anything to her, Jimmy?"

The clerk nodded. "I said that at this time of the year it was unlikely that you would be at home. I told all the rest of the staff to stick to the same story. I remembered what you told me after . . ." Again he looked uncertainly at Fred. ". . . the last occasion. You know, Colonel. Last year when that other woman claimed . . ."

Ned produced several dollars and shoved them in Jimmy's hand. "Quite so, quite so. You are a good fellow, Jimmy. I think in this instance that discretion might be the better part of valor, as the great William Shakespeare once said."

"In Henry IV, Part One, I believe," said Fred, keen to hear that Ned was choosing to avoid a possible altercation with two "capable" looking men.

"Quite so, good Fred. Now come, we must away with all speed."

Jimmy caught Ned's arm. "Colonel, the one

thing you ought to know is this. The lady is telling everyone that she is Mrs. Judson—your wife."

Ned stared at Jimmy and seemed to teeter on his feet. Fred Pond put a hand on his elbow to steady him.

"But Mrs. Judson is back home at the Eagle's Nest," Fred said. "I don't understand."

Ned recovered himself. "Of course she is, Fred. There is some mistake here, this is someone's idea of a sick joke."

There was the sound of a wooden step creaking behind them and they all three looked round to see that a large burly-looking fellow wearing a bowler hat and an ill-fitting, over-tight suit was standing with a foot on the bottom step.

"There ain't no mistake and this is no joke," he said, pointing past them.

"Colonel Judson," came a deep voice from the hotel doorway. "Our employer will be obliged if you would step inside."

Ned looked around slowly and appraised the second speaker. Like the man on the bottom step he was well built, weather-beaten and rugged. From the shape of his nose and the thickness of his ears he was clearly a veteran of many bare-knuckle fights.

"I am afraid I must decline your invitation, gentlemen. I never accept offers of hospitality from strange women, for if you two are the sort of company she keeps, she must be strange indeed."

"It warn't no invitation," said the man on the bottom step.

"And we don't take kindly to a pipsqueak like you calling our employer a strange woman."

The bottom step man stepped onto the next step. "No, she's a lady and—"

His words were cut short as Ned's stick suddenly was swept in an arc, its heavy head picking up considerable momentum to collide with his groin. He gasped as his hands went to his genitals and he doubled up. But he didn't complete the doubling, for Ned's heel flicked up with some force in time to catch him on the chin, causing him to hurtle backwards to land sprawled in the dust. Instantly, he screamed and doubled up to begin retching his guts up.

Fred heard the man at the doorway curse at the unexpected resistance of their quarry. As he glanced around he saw the fellow drop into a fighting posture, a hand reaching for a gun at his hip. "Colonel! Watch out—"

But Ned was already on the move. No sooner had he kicked the first man down the steps, he swept his stick round and unsheathed the sword.

"Have at you, ye varlet!" he cried, lunging forward and deftly rapping the man's knuckles with the flat of the blade.

To Fred it was as if he was suddenly watching

one of Alexander Dumas' Three Musketeers, or even one of Ned Buntline's own novels about *The Knight of the Black Shield.*

The man bellowed in pain and withdrew his hand from his holstered weapon. "You dirty little—" he began, taking a step toward Ned. "Now I'm gonna kill you."

But displaying considerable lightness of foot and surprising dexterity for one who had been hobbling for all the time that Fred had known him, Ned wielded his sword to prod, prick and whip his adversary, who suddenly cowered backwards under the tirade of blows that he was powerless to defend against.

Finally, moving in, while still prodding and whipping with his sword, Ned grabbed the man's handgun and tossed it backwards into the street.

"A word of advice, sir," said Ned. "Never threaten a man unless you have the ability to carry out those threats."

The man growled as he tried to protect himself with his arms.

"And that is enough of a lesson for today," said Ned, flamboyantly sheathing his sword in his stick and returning the tip to the floor with an emphatic click.

The man wasted no time, but charged at Ned, who side-stepped adroitly and swiftly brought the head of his cane down on the man's head. Then with a contemptuous kick he expelled him from the stoop to land heavily beside his companion, who continued to rub his bruised groin and retch.

Almost inevitably, a crowd of passers-by and assorted town loafers had congregated at the sound of a brawl. Many started laughing at the discomfiture of the two dust covered bodyguards.

"Don't you know who you tangled with?" cried one.

"That's our Colonel Judson," said another.

"If you'd known it was Ned Buntline you'd have stayed at home," cried another, much to Ned's obvious pleasure.

Turning to Jimmy, Ned beamed, all but swaggering in front of the audience that had gathered. "Please pass on my regards to this mysterious lady and tell her that I am unavailable. I and my young friend, biographer and literary agent, Fred Pond here have a train to catch. I am heading on a lecture tour beginning in Chicago. It is all arranged."

Fred stared open mouthed at the two large men retching and panting in the dust, who had been dealt with so spectacularly by Ned. He pointed to them. "Colonel Judson, shouldn't we—?"

Ned had swiftly descended to the street and unhitched his horse. "No, Fred, we shouldn't. We have a train to catch and we will have to hurry." He mounted his horse with more vigor than he had shown before.

Fred followed suit, carefully avoiding the two

men who were slowly recovering, but still looked dangerous, even if less capable than before.

"Remember, Jimmy," said Ned, his voice raised almost to the point of shouting. "We have to catch the train. Chicago beckons."

He was about to turn his mount when the doors of the hotel opened and a striking woman in a black dress with a bustle and wearing a black toque with a dark veil sauntered out, clutching a large, black, purse string bag. She seemed slightly unsteady on her feet.

Not surprising, thought Fred. If Jimmy was telling the truth she'd been drinking whiskey all day.

"Not so damned fast, Ned-rot-your-hide-Buntline," she said, sweeping her veil up to reveal a handsome face with a firm jaw. "You remember me, don't you, husband dear!"

Ned's face paled, but he managed to maintain a stoic, poker countenance. "You have me at a disadvantage, ma'am. I know you not."

"You know me, Ned, or Edward Judson, whatever name you're hiding under right now. I'm Daisy Blanche Buntline, just like it said on those playbills back west. And just like it says on our marriage certificate."

Her hand darted into the purse string bag and pulled out a rolled-up certificate. "You're mine, Ned Buntline and so help me I'm here to get you and all that belongs to me."

Ned raised an eyebrow. "I wish you luck, ma'am. I perceive by your apparel that you have lost someone close. Perhaps your grief has turned your mind a little. Maybe you've read one or two of my books and somehow gotten them all a mite twisted." He smiled smugly and added: "Drinking whiskey has a tendency to pickle one's thoughts."

The crowd was beginning to enjoy the war of words between the mounted Ned and the lady in widow's weeds standing on the hotel stoop. Fred Pond, for his part, was beginning to feel sorry for the woman, whose two bodyguards had staggered to their feet and mounted the steps to stand either side of her.

"You want to know why I'm dressed like this, Ned," she went on. "I'm here because I expect to be a widow real soon." Her hand again disappeared inside the bag and came out a moment later with a Peacemaker clasped in a firm hand. "Now get down from that horse, afore I flick you off it."

Ned stared at her, a momentary look of anxiety flashing across his face. Then he was his usual blustering self. "I would if I could, ma'am. The thing is, you have clearly made a mistake. I am Colonel Edward Judson and I have to go with my companion and literary agent here to catch a train. We must get to Chicago to begin my lecture tour."

The hammer of the gun was ratcheted back in a hand as steady as a rock, at variance with the slight whiskey induced slur in her voice. "Get down from that horse, Ned Buntline and get your ass in here, or I swear I'll be a widow before that train has gone."

The crowd started to edge away from the line of fire and possible stray bullets.

Ned tipped his hat with the head of his cane. "Fare you well, ma'am. I fear that I must leave you with your two bruisers there and your misguided dreams."

There was the explosive noise of a shot and the crowd fell back several yards, dispersing out of self-preservation.

Fred had ducked at the sound but looked up now to see blood trickling down from Ned Buntline's left earlobe. The shoulders of his buckskin jacket were covered in blood. Ned had not moved, albeit his face registered shock. Then almost macabrely, he grinned. "Why, that gun must have just gone off by itself," he said with the utmost nonchalance. Whether it pained him or not, he did not show it. He turned to Fred:

"Come my boy. The train awaits us."

There was another shot and the crowd moved back further, with many cries of alarm, cursing and further gasps of amazement. Surely, this mad woman meant to murder their Colonel Judson.

When people dared to look back they saw blood dripping down from the lobe of his other ear, yet he sat still in his saddle.

"Goodbye, ma'am," said Ned, turning his already frightened horse. He urged it to walk then gradually lope away in the direction of the railroad station.

Fred tremulously followed, albeit not risking getting into the line of sight between Ned and the shooting woman.

The crowd half expected another shot, perhaps one that would hit its mark and tumble Ned from his saddle, but it did not come. Instead, she shouted after him:

"I will get you, Ned Buntline. I'm here for what is mine and I will get you. Do you understand?"

Ned rode on and Fred followed.

She cried even louder. "I said, do you understand? I will have what is mine. You know as well as I do that I always get what I aim at."

Then she fired again, emptying her gun as she fired repeatedly into the air.

Everyone in the crowd, including her two bodyguards had winced and hunkered down, convinced now that she was a woman full of hate and anger.

"Do you reckon she is the colonel's wife?" someone whispered.

"No way," replied another. "You saw the cool way he beat those ruffians up, then let her shoot at him. He's as straight as a die is the colonel. There is no way he'd cheat on Mrs. Judson."

"No, but Ned Buntline might," replied a third.

Fred had caught up with Ned, his mind full of questions, but his immediate concern was more for the blood loss that his writing idol would sustain, to say nothing of his admiration for the way he had dispatched the two bodyguards.

"That woman, she . . . she tried to kill you, Colonel. Your buckskin jacket is ruined."

To his utter surprise Ned laughed as he dabbed at one ear with a blood-soaked handkerchief. "Fear not, dear Fred. A jacket can be replaced, and these are but the merest of flesh wounds. I can barely feel them if you must know. The lobe of the ear bleeds a lot, but it does not hurt overmuch. Had you not wondered why so many of the fairer sex submit themselves to mutilation with ear-rings? The reason is that it hardly hurts at all to pierce the ear."

Fred whistled. "Boy, I was amazed at how you were able to move so quickly, what with your gout and all."

"Ah therein lies one of the great mysteries about the human body, Fred. It is a phenomenon that I have experienced personally many times. A person can have the most dreadful wound, yet in the heat of battle or when one's very existence is in danger, why the mind somehow blocks out the pain. I have ridden a horse for twenty miles with two bullets in my back. Another time I swam across the Rio Grande with a broken leg. It is often some time later that the pain kicks in again."

Both incidents were, of course, figments of Ned's imagination, but delivered with conviction, for he had recounted them so many times that he himself believed their veracity.

"Do they not hurt now, Colonel?"

Ned shook his head as he dabbed at his ears again. "Not one whit, Fred."

"Then it has been a most fortunate outcome, for an inch difference with either shot and you would be dead."

Ned again laughed. "You are correct, Fred. Those bullets couldn't have come closer without doing me real harm. If Daisy Blanche Buntline meant to kill me then I would be lying in the undertaker's being measured for my coffin right now. The truth is, I couldn't have been in safer hands than hers."

"But, you called her Daisy Blanche—Buntline?"

"I did."

Fred gulped. "So, does that mean that you actually were married to her? She was telling the truth?"

"I was. She was telling the truth, for we were man and wife." Then seeing Fred's look of incredulity, he continued. "But not married in the way you think, Fred. It was a sham, a mere game. A ploy between us some years ago. I will tell you about it later. When I am ready to."

He pointed ahead to the station. "Right now, I'd like you to take these horses to the livery. Dan Olsen will recognize them, so just tell him to look after them until I return in a few days. Meanwhile, I will purchase tickets and visit the telegraph office. I have three urgent telegrams that I must send before the train comes."

He patted his saddle bags. "A lesson for you, Fred. Always pack a spare set of clothes lest you suffer injuries such as Daisy Blanche inflicted on me. I will change clothes and see if I can tend to my ears in the station master's office. He is another fine fellow and will oblige me."

A mere ten minutes later they were sitting opposite each other in the first-class car on the Ulster and Delaware railroad.

Ned had transformed his appearance from his buckskins and was wearing a good quality, if rumpled blue fatigue suit of the army, with a blue coat, brass buttons and upon his lapels several medals.

His ear lobes were covered in some sort of padding and bandages, which he had attempted to conceal as best he could by pulling his hair down over them. It was only a partial success and he stood out among the other first-class passengers, many of whom muttered greetings like old friends, further testimony to Ned Buntline's widespread fame.

"Sit back and enjoy the trip through the Catsgills, Fred. We are twenty-five miles from Arkville, where we can pick up the New York, Ontario and Western toward New York. There we could change for the New York Central and thence west to Chicago."

Fred had started to make notes in his book, but looked up in surprise. "Chicago? We are really heading for Chicago? But we have no luggage, Colonel."

Ned chuckled as he produced his old yellow oilskin pouch and started to stuff his corncob pipe with tobacco. Then he winked and leaned closer to whisper conspiratorially.

"That is entirely what I have told everyone, Fred. When Daisy Blanche arrives at the station with her two hapless ruffians that is precisely what they will be told by Albert the stationmaster and by Finn Drake the telegraphist. Good men, they will not give us away, for they have been well remunerated. With good fortune Daisy Blanche and her minions will hope to catch us before the connecting train arrives at Arkville."

"So, they have a chance of catching us at Arkville, Colonel?"

Ned struck a light and puffed his pipe into

action. "No, because we will not be there. We will stay on the train all the way to Kingston, which is fifty miles further on."

"And then catch the New York Central to Chicago?"

Ned shook his head. "No, Fred. We shan't catch it. Instead, we'll disembark at Rondout and head for the Hudson. I have a single-handed cruiser there, which I often take out on the Hudson. By the time we arrive there will be fresh stores and supplies ready and waiting for us. That was the first of my telegrams."

Fred Pond's eyes lit up. "We're going sailing." Then he looked concerned. "But what about Mrs. Buntline? That is, the real Mrs. Buntline who must be fretting right now back in the Eagle's Nest."

Ned blew a series of smoke rings toward the roof of the car. "My second telegram was to Hazel Eyes. She will know that we have been called away urgently, on an adventure. Don't worry, Fred. She is used to receiving such missives, for she is the wife of a writer and she understands that I often must fly to follow up a story."

"Where will we be sailing to, Colonel?"

Ned blew a stream of smoke and then pouted. "Who knows? The Hudson is the greatest river on Earth, Fred. It has played important parts in my life, from my hunting days in the Adirondacks. Then as a young man I spent six months as a fur trapper in the Hudson Bay. I learned the ways of the beaver and eventually could even think like one, so I knew their vulnerability. I became one of the Hudson Bay Company's finest procurers of fur. My novel about *Beaverskin Rattry and the Lost City of Gold* was pretty much autobiographical."

Fred stared incredulously. "Gold, Colonel. You don't mean that there really is a city—?"

Ned gave a short laugh and waved his pipe dismissively. "Poetic license, Fred. Or we may just tarry and drop our fishing lines. I know places where I can promise fine fishing."

Fred nodded and settled back to enjoy the views as the train chugged along through the valleys and over the hills of the majestic Catskills Mountains. He was content to be going fishing, his favorite pastime, but also excited to be on an adventure with his hero, Colonel Edward Judson. As his eyes closed and he drifted into sleep he saw himself as a character, a heroic figure in his very own novel penned by Ned Buntline.

Chapter 6

THE CAPTAIN'S PIG AND THE MAN O'WAR

Rondout Harbour at the mouth of Rondout Creek was a revelation to Fred. Both sides of the creek were lined by all manner of businesses, from brickworks, tanneries, seed and grain merchants, iceworks and not least, the huge Cornell Steamboat Company. The whole area was busy with a variety of river traffic. Barges, steamboats, sloops, ketches and the odd cutter covered the water, and the wharfs buzzed with trade as cargos were loaded or unloaded by stevedores and porters. Old salts sat outside warehouses and taverns, swapping tales and passing the day smoking and drinking coffee, beer or rum.

"There is a constant stream of traffic down to New York all day, carrying both passengers and cargoes," said Ned, leading the way to a row of chandleries and boat repair yards where many private crafts were moored up. "We, however, are headed the other direction."

They stopped in front of a sleek, 35-foot cruiser, which had an intriguing, if somewhat ostentatious figurehead on its bow. It was of a pig wearing a captain's cap.

"Welcome to *The Captain's Pig*," Ned said,

skipping aboard. "As you see, it's got a cabin with two berths, so go in and explore. Mind your head, though, it's only five feet headroom. Perfectly adequate for an old sailor like me, but landlubbers might struggle a mite."

Fred Pond laughed. "You've already taken to speaking like a sea-going man, Colonel."

Ned nodded. "You may have noticed, Fred, I adapt to whatever place I'm in. It always pays off. Now do as I suggest and check the cabin while I go and settle up with my good friend Daniel Kennedy, the chandler."

Fred did as he was bidden and checked out the cabin, which was about nine-foot-long and about four and a half feet wide. He crept in, bending as low as he could and tested the berths, which were a tad harder than he would have liked. He wondered how he would fare with the closeness of cabin walls, for he had never enjoyed enclosed spaces ever since the day that his father had locked him in a cupboard as a punishment for going fishing instead of going to school.

Yet restricted though the space was, it had a coal stove, cooking gear, wall lockers and fishing tackle on hooks on the walls. He looked inside the various lockers and found them well stocked with tins, boxes and bottles of water and also some bottles of beer.

"Are we heading straight off?" he asked after Ned had paid the chandler who had fulfilled his request by telegram. Ned told him that he had also as a gesture of good will to the merchant signed a pile of his dime novels, thereby increasing their value at least fourfold.

"Indeed we are, Fred. We must go before too many people discover that Ned Buntline is in their midst. As you know, I have a surprisingly large following among men of the sea and the waters, on account of several of my maritime dime novels. Once again discretion is needed, for on the off chance that Daisy Blanche pursues us here we don't want anyone telling her that we've taken to the water."

It did not take long for Ned to ready the cruiser. The very first thing he did was to raise the Old Glory and salute it. Fred followed suit.

"It is my custom to fly the flag wherever I go, Fred. Whether that is on the water, in a hotel room or back in my own home in the Eagle's Nest, I hoist Old Glory. An American should always be proud to fly the flag. So many of our fathers, brothers and sons died for this country, first to free the Thirteen Colonies from the British yoke, then during the Civil War. It is only right to honor them and this great country that they fought and died for."

Fred nodded in the direction of the cabin hatch. "I see we are well provided for, Colonel."

Ned nodded, then eyed Fred askance. "You can swim, can't you, Fred?"

"Assuredly, Colonel. Every fisherman should know how to save himself."

The novelist patted his shoulder. "That's good. I was just checking. When you go on the water you should always remember the three 'S's. That is safety, shelter and sustenance. *The Captain's Pig* is as safe as they come, but you being able to swim is reassuring, for one never knows what can happen on the Hudson. Our cabin will give us all the shelter we shall need, and Daniel has stocked us up with sustenance."

Fred had produced his notebook and jotted down Ned's nugget of wisdom about the three 'S's.' He was sure that the colonel would have tales to tell for each letter. He made a note to follow up on this later.

They cast off and Fred watched as Ned showed his expertise on the water. Everything he did was done with precision and seemed second nature. Whenever he stood up and moved about, it was clear that he had instantly found his sea legs again. The cruiser's sails billowed in the wind and he expertly maneuvered the tiller to move it past and around vessels of all sizes, as it cut through the water.

It was apparent also that *The Captain's Pig* was well known, as was its owner on the great river. Ships hooted or honked as they passed, while pilot or passengers waved and called out.

"Ahoy, Colonel Judson."

"Good day, Colonel Buntline!"

"Howdy, Ned!"

Others merely pointed at the figurehead and made hog like snorts and jackknifed with laughter before heartily waving at them.

Fred was struck that almost everywhere they went people recognised the writer and knew him by a variety of names. Almost everywhere he seemed to be regarded with almost universal affection. It was also abundantly clear that he reveled in his celebrity.

"So why is the cruiser called *The Captain's Pig*?" Fred ventured.

Ned Buntline looked at him in amazement. "You mean I hadn't told you before? *The Captain's Pig* was the title of my first ever published work. It was about an amusing little happening when I was a commissary for the midshipmen on a man o' war. At Vera Cruz I and the commissioned officer's commisary each bought three little pigs and stowed them in separate crates on deck, ready for slaughter during the voyage. As bad luck would have it as we sailed to Havana we hit a squall and one crate was washed overboard. The other broke, but two of the piglets also got swept away."

Fred made notes. "So, there was just one left?"

"That's right. A little fellow with a black spot over one eye. I knew it was ours for the use of the midshipmen, but the officer's commissary claimed it was his, for the officers. The captain came down from the bridge when he heard our heated argument. He listened, then ordered that it was to be saved for the captain's table. Well, that wasn't fair and I saw red, Fred!"

"With just cause, I would say, Colonel."

"Well, the pig was duly killed and roasted, but when the officer's commissary went to call the captain and officers to the table, I and a couple of my fellows took the said spitting pig and made off with it to the midshipmen's mess, where we proceeded to have a fine if somewhat hasty meal. When the captain and his officers stormed along the deck after they had found their pig had disappeared, all they found were us middies leaning against bulwarks, picking our teeth. Suffice to say that the captain was furious, but no one admitted to having even seen a pig, let alone eaten some of it. It kept the lads amused for weeks and I couldn't resist writing the story up. Of course, I did not dare use my own name, hence Ned Buntline the author came into being."

He patted the tiller. "When I bought this little beauty of a cruiser there was only one name for it. *The Captain's Pig.*"

They cruised past the old Rondout bluestone lighthouse and then past the Esopus Meadows. Ned explained that it was called that because at low tide the mud flats were only a foot or two underwater. The lighthouse had been built there to keep mariners away for fear of running aground.

On the banks dense woodlands had here and there been cleared to build huge mansions and estates for some of the wealthiest of American families.

"I've often thought of building a house here on the Hudson, myself," mused Ned. "Then I decided against it, for I could hardly have a more comfortable home than the Eagle's Nest. Besides, I can cruise wherever I want in *The Captain's Pig* and anchor or moor where the fancy takes me. I like comfort, Fred, but when I am on the Hudson I like the freedom to fish or go hunting."

During a couple of pleasant hours sailing, enjoying the feel of the fresh air on their faces and the smell of the water and of the forests that adorned the banks of the river, Ned regaled Fred with anecdotes of the places he had been and the many adventures he had enjoyed on his trips on the Hudson.

As the evening shadows came Ned made for one of the many islands on the Hudson and moored *The Captain's Pig*.

"I often come to this one and kind of think of it as my own private isle. It's big enough to hide away from the river traffic and it has shelter, plenty of wood and also has some great spots to fish from." He disappeared into the cabin and came out a few moments later with two rods and some cans of bait.

"We could have jerky or pemmican, but I wager that between us we can produce a haul of fish fit for a king's table."

Fred grinned and took the proffered rod. "You mean for the captain's table, don't you, Colonel?" he asked with a grin. "Well now, it is my turn to show you that an editor doesn't spend all of his time behind a desk. Let's dine in style."

Choosing a couple of spots to cast from it did not take long before between them they had landed a couple of striped bass, a large bluefish and a weakfish with its distinctive yellow and orange fins.

Ned built a fire and soon the air was full of the aroma of griddled fish.

"What is your view on strong drink, Fred?" Ned asked, returning from *The Captain's Pig* with a hamper.

"I am partial to an occasional beer or small glass of wine, Colonel. I even have to admit that when I go fishing I take a hip flask of spirits. I hadn't wanted to mention it before, knowing your own strong views on the demon drink."

"Ah yes, it is true that I include tracts on temperance in my novels. And I have given more lectures on it than Ulysses S. Grant had victories, but the truth is that I myself occasionally permit myself to drink hard liquor. It is only by imbibing that you can see the evils of drink and thence can speak more effectively and authoritatively about it."

Fred nodded as he turned the trout on the griddle over the fire. "I can see your logic, Colonel. So, if you have some of Mrs. Buntline's lemonade in that hamper then I am more than happy."

Ned shook his head with a smile. "Not on this occasion, I am afraid. Since this is by way of being an adventure of sorts I thought it would be one of those times when I would relax my temperance habit. I have beer and I have some of the finest rye whiskey. The beer will wash the fish down and the whiskey will create the right mood for tales under the stars by the warmth of the campfire."

The food did indeed go down well, and the beer had created a warm feeling inside Fred Pond. Sitting cross-legged opposite Ned Buntline, the author of a veritable mountain of dime novels and magazine articles he felt like a disciple sitting at the feet of an intellectual giant.

After their third whiskey Fred was aware that it took an effort to prevent his voice from slurring. He poked the fire, causing sparks to rise and the embers to crackle. He asked:

"How long do you feel we will need to stay away from the Eagle's Nest, Colonel?"

117

"A day or two, Fred. Apart from the fishing and sailing I have it in mind to pen a novel. The idea came to me last night and this affords a suitable opportunity for you to watch how I write. Whether that is going to be of the remotest use to you or any of your readers is another matter entirely."

Fred sat forward eagerly. "Are you saying that you have a method of writing?"

"I do, Fred and it is a fairly simple process that has held me in good stead over several hundred novels and several thousand articles, essays and newspaper columns."

He smiled, raised his glass and drained it in one swallow. "First, I come up with a title. Then I picture my main characters and the sort of novel it will be. Almost invariably it will be an adventure with a strong romantic component. It will always have a powerful moral message, usually about the evils of too much strong drink, or the hazards of gambling, or just man's inhumanity to his fellow beings."

Fred suddenly sniggered. "I've noticed that. It's sometimes a bit incongruous to have the action suddenly stall halfway through, while the hero rails against something. Why, Colonel, it's sometimes downright funny."

Ned was not at all put out by his biographer's reaction. Instead he reached over with his bottle and topped up both their glasses.

"Of course, it may seem incongruous, my boy. Sometimes even humorous, as I intended it should. Yet for all that, the soliloquy is a literary device that was used by no less a genius than William Shakespeare. Remember Macbeth's soliloquy? I saw our late, great actor Edwin Forrest playing several roles including Macbeth when he was in his prime and acknowledged as the best tragedian actor in the whole world."

He jumped up, his face aglow in the light from the fire. His expression suddenly changed to one of amazement and wonder as he reached into the air as if something floated in front of him. Then in a booming, melodramatic voice:

"Is this a dagger which I see before me, the handle towards my hand. Come, let me clutch thee."

Fred applauded. "Wonderful, Colonel. More, please."

With barely a pause Ned pulled himself straight and adopted a haughty, nose in the air attitude. "To be, or not to be, that is the question. Whether 'tis nobler in the mind to suffer the slings and arrows of outrageous fortune . . ."

He glanced down at Fred. "Edwin Forrest played that part as well. Do you know who said those words, my boy?"

"Hamlet, Prince of Denmark, Colonel."

Ned nodded and slumped back down and picked up his glass. "Quite right. Those two soliloquys tell us a lot about the characters in the plays. In the first one Shakespeare has Macbeth struggle with his conscience as he imagines a murderous dagger before him. He is wary of it, yet if he follows the path his mind is showing, he could have power. He could be king."

He drained his glass and gestured for Fred to do likewise. Fred Pond duly did, and immediately coughed as the fiery liquid burned his throat before hitting his stomach.

"Then in Hamlet," Ned went on, in full lecture mode, "Hamlet is talking about life and death and the cruel things that life can throw at one. I love that soliloquy, Fred. It is so true about life. It can throw slingshot and arrows at you. Yes, and musket balls, bullets and knives, too."

He laughed and pulled out his corncob pipe. "I read those lines in my father's library when he would have had me reading legal texts instead. But I just thought that Shakespeare knew more than all the fusty judges and lawyers who wrote the law. His words made an impact on me then, Fred. I chose to attack life from that moment and I've never stopped. I have been in dangerous situations all my life and came through every one of them, because I always kept moving on. I have lived my life as if I am the main character in a wonderful play. I may not always keep to the script, for I am given to improvising, to ad-libbing. I think that gets me into trouble, but equally I have been able to extricate myself from many tight spots by my wits, my tongue and my quick actions."

Fred snapped his fingers. "You're soliloquizing right now, in a way, aren't you, Colonel. I see how you do all that in your novels. So, go on, sir and tell me more of your writing method."

Ned poured more whiskey. "Ah yes, well, conflict is next, Fred. I may have my heroine abducted by a villain, so a chase is begun. My hero, always a man of brains as well as brawn, gives chase, but will be thwarted by ill luck, or by some nefarious actions by the villain and his countless henchmen. He will be wounded, shot at, beaten, but despite everything he will prevail. Love, a powerful emotion will motivate him to brave the very fires of hell to get his loved one back."

Fred's head was spinning and his image of Ned was growing hazy through the hot air that rose from the fire. He knew that the whiskey was going to his head, but he was enjoying listening to his mentor.

"How important is temp . . . temper . . . temperance to you, Colonel?" He sniggered again as his own difficulty in enunciating words struck him as hilarious. "I mean, here we are, camped by the Hudson, drinking strong liqu . . . liquor while you tell me how you write your novels."

"It is very important, Fred. But as I indicated

before, you have to experience strong drink every now and then in order to understand its hazards. The truth is that some people have no problem with temptation of any sort. They are saints. I am not a saint and I admit that I have been tempted in wrong ways. I have yielded to temptation in many ways, yet I have never allowed any vice to rule me. I can overcome, I can walk away from tobacco, liquor, from the doves of the saloons and dance halls."

Fred stared at him for a moment as he tried to take in what Ned had just said. "You . . . you mean," he began, his voice now deeply slurred. "You mean . . . that you—?"

He was holding his glass halfway to his lips, but his fingers suddenly lost the power to grip it and it fell and bounced off the ground, spilling the contents into the fire, which instantly flared as the liquor erupted in fire.

Fred Pond began to laugh as he looked at Ned Buntline through what seemed to be a conflagration.

"The fires . . . of hell!" he slurred as he fell sideward. He was asleep before his head even hit the ground.

Birds were singing in the trees overhead and a fire was crackling away when Fred slowly came to consciousness next morning. Dimly he realized that he was out of doors, wrapped in a heavy blanket. His mouth felt as dry as the desert sands and his tongue stuck to the roof of his mouth. His bladder felt as if it could burst, but he dared not move, for his head pounded. Gingerly, he opened first one eye, then the other, each causing him to blink as the light of day seared the backs of his eyes.

He lay still for a moment longer with his eyes tightly closed, while he tried to work out what the scratching noise was that assailed his ears.

Then images and memories of the night before came to him, bit by bit. A meal by the campfire, whiskey drinking and yet more whiskey drinking as he listened to Ned Buntline tell him about how he wrote. There were dim memories of Ned reciting from Shakespeare, then some sort of revelation, then—nothing!

What was the scratching sound? It seemed vaguely familiar, yet he could not place it in his current state of befuddlement.

The scratching suddenly stopped and Ned's ever cheerful voice sounded like thunder to Fred's hypersensitive state.

"Ah, you are awake at last. Open your eyes, good Fred, for it is a good day to be alive."

Fred forced himself to stir, painfully managing to prop himself up on an elbow as he prized his eyes open to focus on the writer, who closed a notebook and stowed away a pencil that he had been writing with. He pointed to two large dead birds lying beside him with a catapult alongside them.

"I have been at work the last two hours while you slumbered on. I went hunting and caught a brace of pigeons, which will serve for our dinner tonight."

"You killed them with that?" Fred asked in amazement, before wincing as he felt a stab of pain in his head.

"I did indeed. I thought that gunshots might wake you too rudely, so I chose one of the silent hunting weapons of my childhood."

A large steamboat passed by and sounded its steam-whistle as *The Captain's Pig* was spotted by someone on board. Both Ned and Fred waved back at the crew and the dozens of passengers who had come onto the decks to see why the whistle had been sounded. Fred waved weakly and then clapped a hand over his mouth as he strove to avoid retching.

"I fear I over imbibed last night Colonel," he said once the vessel had passed. "I feel like death warmed up."

Ned grinned at him. "Assuredly, you did drink a good deal, Fred, despite my pleas for moderation, but yet you were enjoying yourself. I fear that you have woken with a mighty hangover."

Fred nodded and felt a wave of nausea rise inside him and his stomach began to lurch. He just found enough strength to heave himself up in order to charge into the trees to retch and empty his stomach before finding greater privacy to empty his bladder.

When he unsteadily returned he was relieved that the nausea had lessened, but his head still pounded.

"What you need is a Buntline Man O'War followed by a good hearty breakfast of bacon and eggs," said Ned gathering up the pigeons and heading for the cruiser. He darted across the gangplank more steadily than Fred was used to seeing him. Clearly the gout that had been troubling him had gone.

Yet at the thought of fried food his stomach flipped and he wondered if he would have to retreat into the woods again. "I think perhaps I should pass on breakfast, Colonel," he called as Ned disappeared into the cabin.

Ned's muffled voice called back. "Nonsense. I have the supplies and I am preparing the Man O'War this instant. You just stoke the fire ready for cooking."

A few minutes later Ned returned with a frying pan, the food and a large glass of a yellow liquid.

"Get the Buntline Man O'War down your throat as quick as you can, Fred. It is not a drink to sip, but to gulp down."

With some suspicion and a good deal of trepidation Fred Pond took the proffered drink and drank it down. He closed his eyes as the concoction hit his stomach, with a number of effects.

First, there was a feeling of fullness, then a burst of heat, followed by a pleasant wave of euphoria.

"Well?" Ned asked. "Has it had any effect?"

Fred beamed at him. "That . . . That is remarkable, Colonel. My head was pounding so much that I thought I'd like to have sawed it off, yet the headache has gone entirely. I feel happy, a bit dizzy, but decidedly more content with life than a few seconds ago."

"What about the queasiness?"

Fred thought for a second then nodded emphatically. "Entirely gone, sir. Why, I think I could even face some breakfast."

Ned had immediately started laying thick bacon rashers on the pan, which started to sizzle.

"I knew it would do the trick. The Man O'War is an invention of mine, consisting of two raw eggs, two fingers of rum, a spoon of molasses, cracked peppercorns, powdered skullcap and a hair of the dog that bit you."

Fred grinned. "You mean I've had more rye whiskey and rum and all that other stuff?"

"You have indeed, Fred. The preparation of cures for hangovers is something that has interested me for years and also goes in line with my temperance work. I have given this to many a drunkard and cured them on the spot of their hangovers, and because they were so amazed and relieved they instantly felt strong enough to take the pledge."

Fred reached into his vest and pulled out his hip flask. "I was going to let you sample some of this last night, before I—er—fell asleep."

Ned took it from him and pulled the cork. "What is it?"

"The finest Glenlivet malt whisky. It comes all the way from the highlands of Scotland."

Ned sniffed it disdainfully and was about to hand it back, but he stayed his hand. "Then I regret that I cannot drink this, Fred. I made a pledge."

"What, you took the pledge after last night?"

Ned laughed heartily. "No, not that sort of pledge, Fred. I made a pledge years ago not to drink this stuff when there is good American liquor to be had. In my view the only use for this Glenlivet or whatever you call it is to fuel the fire."

So saying, he tipped the contents into the fire, producing a roar of blue flames that caused the bacon to sizzle even more. "Now for the eggs," he said, cracking the shells of two at once and dropping them into the pan. "We must eat and then get underway. There is work to be done."

Fred nodded as he licked his lips. Suddenly the thought of breakfast appealed to him more than anything. "Aye, aye, sir," he said in mock nautical tones. "And if you don't mind, there are several questions that I'd like to ask you."

Chapter 7

THE GENIE OF THE HUDSON

Back on the river, Fred sat on the deck sketching in his notebook while Ned sat by the tiller as they cruised before the wind, with the mainsheet well out, so the sail was nearly at right angles with the vessel. A fair artist, Fred had half an idea to illustrate each biographical article with hand drawn portraits of Ned.

Fred watched the novelist operating the tiller with one hand while a pencil in his other hand was darting back and forth across the page of a notebook which rested upon his knee. Once again, the scratching noise that had been present when Fred had wakened that morning was very obvious now as the pencil point left its grey trail of copperplate writing upon the paper.

"You write at breakneck speed, Colonel. How on earth do you manage to think so fast while you are also concentrating on steering the craft?"

Ned gave a short laugh. "You just said it, Fred! Craft is the operative word. I have been sailing and writing so long that they are both crafts that come automatically. Last night when I fear that we both may have over imbibed, I talked about my method of writing. This is it in action." He held the pencil up from the paper and licked the point with his tongue. "This is the easy part; I just let the words flow one after the other. If I am unhappy with the way a piece of writing is coming I just jettison it and start again. I know then that any inadequacies in the first piece will be bypassed in the second."

"Then do you edit it and redraft it?"

"Almost never. One draft is usually the final draft."

"And you write every day?"

"Every day that I wake, Fred. There is always something to write about." He stuffed his pencil into a pocket and drew out his corncob pipe. Reaching over the side he tapped out the cold ashes and then charged it from his pouch, while operating the tiller by lodging it under his arm so that he could free his hands. Striking a light he puffed it contentedly for a few moments, producing voluminous clouds of smoke that dissipated quickly in the breeze.

He picked up a pewter sailor's mug by his side and took a hefty swig of what Fred thought was coffee, but which was in fact corn mash whiskey. He grinned as it hit the spot and replaced his pipe, to produce more smoke.

Fred Pond snapped his fingers and sniggered. "That smoke, it's given me the idea for this little vignette I've drawn of you." He turned the sketch round for Ned to see.

Ned nodded approval. "You have a fine eye, Fred. Although you have a tendency to miss out the odd wrinkle or two. Not that I am complaining, mind you."

Fred turned the pencil lead flat to the paper and emphasized the smoke billows around Ned in the picture. "You are like a genie from the *One Thousand and One Nights*, Colonel. Have you read the book?"

"Of course I have. My father had a copy of Edward William Lane's translation in his library. I devoured it when I was a lad when I was supposed to be reading law books." He laughed. "A genie, eh? Like in *Aladdin and His Magic Lamp*."

"That pewter mug you just drank from put the idea into my head. It's like the magic lamp from which you produce these marvelous stories."

"I never really thought about it, but I suppose that book helped to stimulate the writer in me. I certainly loved the exotic adventures in it. Sinbad the Sailor, Ali Baba and the Forty Thieves. I've written about umpteen characters like them. So many of my buccaneering tales feature characters like Sinbad. *Barnacle Backstay*, *The Buccaneer's Daughter*, *The King of the Sea*—I could go on and on."

His eyes grew wistful as he stared ahead, almost as if he was seeing those characters in his mind's eye. He clicked his tongue. "But a genie

I shall be for you, Fred Pond. You said that you had questions for me? Well, like a genie I shall give you three questions and promise to answer them truthfully during the rest of the voyage."

He winked at his biographer and added: "But be sure to choose the questions well, for you are only allowed three!"

"And what would happen if I ask a fourth, Colonel?"

Ned guffawed and adopted a deep melodramatic voice. "Why then I may swat you like a fly and toss you into the Hudson." He winked. "Or maybe I just won't reply."

Fred Pond laughed and pushed his wire-rimmed spectacles back on his nose. "Very well, genie of the Hudson, three questions it will be. The first comes immediately to my mind after sampling that rye whiskey, which we may have had more than was good for us. Simply, how come you have such a reputation as a teetotaler and a temperance lecturer?"

Ned smiled and tapped one of the medals on his lapel. "See this, Fred. This is the Grand Order of the L. N. Fowler Society of Daughters of Temperance, given to me by the good ladies of Manhattan after I gave a lecture and signed the pledge. Lorenzo Fowler, if you didn't know it, is one of the world's foremost experts in phrenology. He is a great advocate of temperance and he drafted the pledge himself."

Fred looked surprised. "I didn't know that, Colonel. But, do you mean you actually took the pledge to give up drinking? And yet—"

"And yet I occasionally imbibe a little?" Ned cut in. He clicked his tongue. "Well, to tell the truth, I signed the paper, but I had my fingers crossed as I did. You see Fred, drinking is all about control. I have control, whereas many don't. That is why I allowed myself to sign the pledge with fingers crossed. You do know that crossing the fingers means you aren't telling a lie?"

He grinned and took a hefty swig from his mug. He recollected the lecture that he gave although not the title, for he had in fact been drinking throughout the preceding night at 77 Lispenard Street, a popular Manhattan brothel which he occasionally frequented in order to gain salacious copy for a newspaper piece he was writing. Along with articles about temperance he had a regular column in which he railed against the dangers of gambling. He reveled in revealing which local dignitaries or high profile gamblers went there to enjoy the pleasures of the flesh.

He laughed inwardly. Sure, I cannot tell young Fred Pond this. He needs a more sanitized version. Wiping his mustache:

"When I ran away to sea as an eleven-year-old boy I saw drinking and drunkenness in abundance. Seafaring men generally like their liquor whenever they hit land. I never saw much sense in it when I was a youngster, drinking to make your mind go numb, your limbs go all rubbery and your tongue to utter the most arrant nonsense. Then to feel awful the next day."

Fred nodded agreement. "Like I did this morning?"

"Exactly! As a young man I found the world too full of adventure to risk numbing my mind, so I tended only to be an occasional imbiber. You see, I knew that I had a literary life ahead of me and I devoted my spare time to writing. When I moved to Pittsburgh I set up my first magazine, *Ned Buntline's Magazine*. I actually did it with my father, whom I had temporarily reconciled with at that time."

Plus, Ned thought, I needed his money to do so.

"Was this magazine a precursor of the famous *Ned Buntline's Own*?"

"It was and we had it printed by Robinson & Jones of Cincinnati, whom my father had published with before. The magazine did very well indeed. I wrote stories, articles and reviews. In the second issue I reviewed a book called *Six Nights with the Washingtonians*, by Timothy Shay Arthur, a young writer who was championing the temperance movement. It was about the Washington Temperance Society that had been set up by half a dozen alcoholics. They advocated total abstinence and they each gave the others the support and strength they needed to defeat their craving for alcohol. Anyway, young Tim Arthur convinced me that it was a good thing. I attended some lectures and because of my penetrating questions from the floor I was invited to speak. Before I knew it, I was being heralded as the temperance lecturer to book, because I would be guaranteed to get more people than anyone else to sign the pledge."

Picking up and lighting his pipe Ned stared through the rising smoke as he worked the tiller.

"And *Ned Buntline's Magazine* became a mouthpiece for the temperance movement. Ever since then I tend to drop the seeds of temperance into my articles, stories and plays. They always seem popular."

Ned smiled, raised his mug and drained it, suddenly realizing that there seemed to be two Freds sitting watching him and that he was finding it slightly hard to concentrate on the tiller. He yawned.

"Perhaps you'd care to take charge of *The Captain's Pig* for a while, good Fred," he said. "I suddenly find myself rather tired and feel that a short nap would restore me. You'll enjoy the way she handles. You can manage the sails, I'm sure."

Fred moved with alacrity and took Ned's place. "I'll certainly look after her. Where should I make for, Colonel?" he asked as Ned unsteadily made it to the cabin.

"Just follow the river, Fred. After all you can't take *The Captain's Pig* ashore, can you?"

They both laughed at the thought.

Ned was still chuckling to himself in the cabin as he replenished his mug with corn mash whiskey. He drained it and then slumped onto his berth, where he started to snore almost as soon as his head hit the pillow.

Ned eventually resurfaced feeling refreshed and somewhat sobered, albeit quite red in the face. He took over from Fred and they sailed up through Putnam County around the great S-curve of the Hudson, passing on the west bank the foundries of Cold Spring.

"That's where they made the Parrott rifled artillery guns they used in the war," Ned said, sniffing the air. "It smells, doesn't it? Well, that's like nothing compared to when a line of these were firing twenty pounders in the field. I didn't like them much, on account of I saw too many explode and burst apart."

"Did you see a lot of action in the war, Colonel?" Fred asked.

"Too much," replied Ned. "On the battlefields of Bull Run, Shiloh and Gettysburg, and countless sorties when I was chief of scouts. Yet the one that made most impact upon me, and which won me a medal for gallantry, occurred not long after I entered the war. Although friends in high places had offered me a commission, I wanted no privilege. Accordingly, in 1862 I enlisted as a private in the First New York Mounted Rifles. It was not long, of course, before I was promoted to sergeant, but the event I am talking about occurred when I was still a private.

"I reached the regiment and immediately a reconnaissance was ordered to feel the enemy on the lines of the Blackwater River, and to make a push toward Petersburg to see what their strength was. There was a brigade of infantry under General Wessels; a section of battery L, regular United States artillery under Lieutenant Beecher; the howitzer battery of First Mounted Rifles under Fairgraves and the First Mounted Rifles under Colonel Dodge.

"I can see Richard Dodge now, Fred. Six foot two and as imposing a figure as you could ever see. He had more charisma than George Armstrong Custer and in my opinion, also had a much better military brain. It was no surprise to me that he would become a general when he was only twenty-three years old.

"Anyway when within half a mile of Black-water Bridge the command was halted in a depression near a stream, scouts were sent ahead and the enemy was found in force across the Blackwater with a long range of masked rifle pits beyond the abutments of the bridge, which, with the steam sawmill at that point, they had burned."

Fred Pond had been sharpening his pencil and tossing the shavings overboard. So enthralled was he that he scarcely noticed when he nicked his own thumbnail. "I can almost see the scene as you describe it, Colonel."

"Private, Fred! Remember I was just a private when you recount this." He grinned and gave a salute. "Colonel Dodge called for a volunteer and without hesitation I stepped forward, stood at attention and saluted him. 'Excellent, Private Judson. I want you to go down and find out exactly where the enemy line is,' says he. So I took a horse and made my way.

"I gained the river bank above the ruins of the mill, rode down to the water's edge and skirted along the shore to the east abutment of the bridge, without seeing a man, or anything but a thick growth of bushes on the high bank just beyond the river. I reckoned it must have been very deep at that point and around a hundred or a hundred and thirty feet wide. The bridge had been a wooden structure with a single span.

"Just as I reached the foot of the abutments, a Confederate officer rose from the bushes and shouted at me: "Halt, you damned Yank! Halt and surrender!"

"Not much!" I replied. We were almost in pistol shot, and all was so still an ordinary voice was audible. I think I hurled back a curse or two. Certainly enough to insult him. As a result, he cried out to fire upon me."

Fred's lower jaw was hanging ever lower.

"At that, every bush seemed to have covered a man, for a full two hundred riflemen poured a concentrated volley on me. The depression from the high bank to where I sat in my saddle was a full thirty degrees, and every shot went over my head. The air seemed hot with bullets, but not one hit me or my horse. But the way that horse went over the bank and out of range was a marvel to behold.

"To ride back, report to the commanding officer, and get to the Mounted Rifles was quick work. The men were all relieved to see me return unscathed and, I admit, they were somewhat heartened to see how excited I was by my adventure."

Fred whistled. "Two hundred guns and not a graze! Incredible, Colonel."

Ned waved a hand. "So, the Thirty-ninth Illinois and the Twenty-sixth Ohio were ordered forward as a skirmish line. Two companies of the Mounted Rifles dismounted, with their Sharps carbines, and two guns of Beechers section of Battery L were sent forward.

"I was given a special squad of sharpshooters

from the Rifles to feel the way, place the artillery and generally do as I thought fit."

Fred gave a laugh. "It shows how valuable they thought you, Colonel."

Ned shrugged nonchalantly. "I gave Beecher his points and showed him two tall trees, which were the limits of the enemy's line as I had seen for myself. Then as the battery galloped to a spot marked by bushes not four hundred yards from the enemy, the infantrymen cautiously advanced under cover in treble skirmish line.

"When I had ridden back I had seen close to the east abutment of the bridge, near a rail fence, a huge sycamore tree. This I judged to be perfect cover. With six men from Company C and two from A, I made a rush for that tree. As we reached it unharmed I made the men lie down and I and two others stood in the ditch behind the trunk and proceeded to start shooting. I ordered the other men to take to loading duty and hand we three shooters a loaded rifle whenever ours were emptied. We were all hidden by the trunk of the tree. The opposite bank was now almost a sheet of fire, though few men could be seen, they were so well masked. Our skirmishers were sending in lead hot and fast.

"Beecher opened fire with his two big Parrott rifle guns. He was firing shrapnel, but his shots went forty feet too high.

"I sent one of my men, Corporal Kane, who

outranked me, but yet had been put in my charge back to tell Beecher how much depression was needed to reach their targets.

"Meanwhile, Lieutenant Wheelan tried to creep through the rail fence to reach my tree, from behind which I was firing as often as I could see a man on the other side. The poor young man never made it, though. He was shot through the throat as he raised his head to speak to me.

"Amid a shower of bullets two of my men, who had kept reloading our guns, caught him and dragged him through the fence and keeping to the tree line, carried him to the rear where I'm sad to say he died minutes later. When I heard that I saw red, for he was but a youngster. Yet all my experience taught me never to let your anger make you rash, for that is the way to get yourself killed. I stayed cool and kept picking off their sharpshooters."

Fred Pond blew air through his lips. "Keeping your cool is a great gift that you have, Colonel. I've seen that for myself when you let Daisy Blanche nick your ears."

Ned laughed. "They will heal up soon enough, Fred. I knew I was in no danger from her. Yet speaking of coolness under fire, I never saw anything to match that of Major William Henry Schieffelin."

Fred snapped his fingers. "I know that name.

Isn't he the top man of Schieffelin & Company, the drug firm in New York?"

"The very man. He was just twenty-five and already the third major of the Mounted Rifles. He had panache in abundance and boy, did he have a cool head. I hadn't realized it at the time, but he had never been in action until that moment. He had ridden up when he heard that young Lieutenant Wheelan had been shot." Ned clicked his tongue. "Well, there he sat in his saddle, his plumed hat over his fair young face, a blue cloak with its red lining thrown back over his shoulder as he curiously watched the enemy at work, just as Beecher's battery started to get the right elevation. As you know, I had been a soldier myself in the Seminole and the Mexican Wars, so I was used to being under fire. I watched him for a few moments with a curiosity and wonder that made me forget any danger to myself, though several bullets grazed me where I stood."

Ned slapped his sides as if he was swatting away gnats or the memory of those bullets that had singed his flesh in the heat of battle.

"Yet there he sat his frightened horse as bullet after bullet whistled over and about him, and he did not seem to mind them a bit, until an officer in the Thirty-ninth Illinois gave him a caution, before he himself was hit a second afterward. 'So this is war, is it?' says he, coolly. 'Rather hot, but they don't kill every shot.' Then he turned

141

his horse and rode slowly back to the battalion.

"Ten minutes later the battery shelled the enemy back, and the Eleventh Pennsylvania cavalry under Colonel Spear came up as a charge had been ordered. Both commands, the Mounted Rifles leading swam the river, captured the enemy's guns, chased their force, which was superior in numbers to ours, as it happened. And then we turned to the right, captured the picket guards at Joiner's Ford seven miles above and joined the infantry at the Isle of Wight court house."

Ned clicked his tongue again. "As we crossed the Blackwater I caught a minié ball in my thigh, although I just kept going. Ahead of me I saw Eugene Boyd, a volunteer surgeon of the One Hundred and Twelfth New York flounder. His horse couldn't swim worth a cent and I had to drag him from the saddle and haul him on my mount. It was fortunate me saving him, for he returned the favor and dug out the minié ball from my leg that afternoon."

"Is that why you sometimes limp on that leg, Colonel? When the gout isn't troubling you, I mean?"

Ned gave one of his guffaws. "I couldn't tell, Fred. When you have taken as many cuts, bullets and arrows as I have, it is hard to link up which pain comes from which old wound."

He looked shoreward at a thick clump of forest.

"I'd like to see that old sycamore tree again. I'll bet if it still stands, and has not yet been hacked down, that twenty pounds of bullets shot at my head and shoulders could be found in that tree."

Fred continued making notes. "Mayhap we should search it out, Colonel. Ned Buntline's sycamore could make a fine photograph."

"Could be that it would," agreed Ned, even though he knew that searching it out would prove difficult. He was not sure himself how much of the tale was true and how much had been conjured up in the telling.

NOTEBOOK 12
Property of Fred E. Pond
Private & Confidential

JOTTINGS ON THE LIFE OF NED BUNTLINE
April 1881

Note 119
The theater lost a great actor when Colonel Judson decided to concentrate on his dime novel writing and his magazines. When he tells one of his anecdotes he delivers it like the accomplished actor that he was. Amazingly, one adventure can lead to several outcomes. His last one resulted in no less than seven dime novels, with *Beadle & Adams*; four of them about the lawmen that had formed a posse to catch a gunman, two about himself and a third a ghost story. I wish at times that I could have lived like the proverbial fly upon the wall and witnessed the events and his actions first hand.

Note 120
Perhaps I am overly suspicious, yet I suspect that the colonel's great imagination sometimes causes him to embellish his tales.

Chapter 8

RADICAL AMERICANISM

Ned pointed ahead. "We'll lay anchor beyond the bend in the river and cook those pigeons I caught."

And so, finding a suitable point close to the bank they prepared to dine. Upon the humble, yet efficient cooking stove in the cabin Ned showed his culinary skills, first plucking the birds and gutting them prior to making a fine stew and dumplings. They ate and drank beer on deck by the light of two oil lamps before Ned picked up his notebook and once again had his pencil pouring words across the page.

When he finally set his writing implements aside Fred was eager to ask his second question.

"Time for question number two, Colonel." He pointed up at Old Glory flying straight in the wind. "You are clearly a patriot, but you seem to have a dislike of all things British. It intrigued me that you would throw away good Scottish malt whisky, like you did this morning for instance. So why this dislike of the British? Is it to do with your youth? You told me that your father wrote about the Revolutionary War."

Ned tapped his teeth with the mouthpiece of his

pipe. It was a question that he suspected might come up at some stage over the course of Fred Pond's visit and he had been considering how much to tell him. He had already decided to give a good edited version to ensure he came out of it well and not in a questionable light.

"No, it was nothing to do with my father. My opinions have always been my own and have usually been forged by my experience of life."

He struck a light to his pipe once again and blew out a stream of smoke. "It is not an easy answer, Fred. You see, I am a man who has suffered much for my views, opinions and convictions. Martyred might be too strong a description, but in a way I was persecuted and I suffered great wrongs as a result."

"What sort of wrongs, Colonel?"

Ned shrugged his shoulders, his face taking on a doleful countenance. "Physical attacks, reputational damage, financial loss, but worst of all, unjustified incarceration."

Fred grimaced. "That is quite a catalogue of wrongs, Colonel." He knew already that Ned had served time in prison, for he had done much research before contacting him in the first place.

"I have been a victim of the law and the penal system more than once, Fred. Both civil law and the harsh military version. Wrongfully each time, I hasten to add."

"And were these incarcerations and injustices

the cause of your dislike of the British and Irish?"

Ned took another swig from his mug and licked his lips. "Don't misunderstand, Fred. It isn't that I dislike the British or the Irish. In fact I have had many British, European and other foreigner friends over the years. As I have told you, I have hunted and shot buffalo with the Russian Grand Duke Alexei Alexandrovich, sailed with an English lord and even played golf, one of the strangest games ever invented with a Scottish champion golfer. All fine fellows as individuals, yet the problem comes when they come over to America in droves and take our jobs. Worse, when they come over and after a couple of years they can become citizens and for some inexplicable reason be allowed to vote in our elections. For these reasons in my youth I joined the Native American Party."

Fred nodded slowly. "So, you were a nativist, Colonel?"

"I never liked the term, Fred," Ned replied with a frown. "I like to think of it as being patriotic and putting Americans first. After all an American has to live his whole life to be a citizen and be able to vote, not be a Johnny-come-lately and get a say in the running of the county, state or country after two years. As I say, I joined the party in the 1840s and quickly rose in the ranks and thanks to my humble talents in public speaking I was asked to campaign many times."

"Wasn't the American Party also called the 'Know Nothing' Party?"

"That was later, in about 1855 after it changed its name from the Native American Party to the American Party. The Know Nothing moniker was a standing joke, which I happened to coin in *Ned Buntline's Own*. It proved popular and the name stuck. Essentially, we ran it rather like the Freemasons, so its origins were in a gentlemen's secret society. We did lots of good works, charitable work, like other such organizations. To avoid outright confrontations and arguments that could be misrepresented and misreported, whenever our members were asked about the details of our party, they were advised to say "I know nothing." Hence we became the Know Nothings."

"What was the Native American Party's stance on slavery, Colonel?"

"Good question, Fred. There was no policy, nothing in the constitution of the Party. Most of the members from the North were in favor of abolition, but many in the South were staunchly against it. To tell you the truth, it was this very matter that saw the party fall apart after our unsuccessful attempt to have Millard Fillmore elected to the presidency of the United States in the 1856 campaign."

Fred made notes as Ned spoke. "I suppose your literary skills came in useful, Colonel?"

A steamer passed with countless lamps illuminating it. As usual, *The Captain's Pig* was recognized by the crew and pointed out to the passengers who hurried to the rails to wave and whistle and call out good intentioned greetings. Ned returned their waves with an enthusiastic and extravagant windmill wave of his own, and Fred, basking in the bonhomie that Ned was continually greeted with, also waved back.

The Captain's Pig gently rose and fell as the great steamer's wheels caused a turbulent wake to spread out over the immediate stretch of the Hudson. Ned lit his pipe again.

"Where was I?" he mused. Then: "Ah yes, my humble writing skills. I closed down *Ned Buntline's Magazine* when I left Pittsburgh and parted company with my father. I arrived in New York in 1846 and started writing in earnest. I was still regularly contributing nautical and autobiographical notes to *Knickerbocker* and a host of other magazines like *Star Spangled Banner* and *Flag of the Union*, but I wanted to become a serious writer of novels. I needed regular income, not just fees for my magazine short stories and articles. *Ned Buntline's Magazine* had been successful, but in New York I was sure that I could produce a bigger, better publication. That's when I conceived the idea for *Ned Buntline's Own*. It was to be a newspaper rather than a magazine. A paper that people could read stories, articles and reviews in, but it had to be different to have an edge on the competitors. It had to be a crusading weekly newspaper. But first I had to make enough money to subsidize it."

He opened another bottle of beer and indicated the case for Fred to help himself to another.

"My first novelette *The Last Days of Calleo, or the Doomed City of Sin* was published by the Jones Publishing House in Boston. It was a best-seller. Soldiers and sailors bought it in droves. A month later Gleason's published *The King of the Sea; A Tale of the Fearless and the Free.* You may be interested to know that I dedicated it to my fellow shipmates from my navy days."

Fred made notes and then reached for his beer.

"The public couldn't get enough of my tales, Fred. I followed these up with *The Queen of the Sea: or Our Lady of the Ocean: A Tale of Love, Strife and Chivalry.* The words came out of me like water. I wrote *Love's Desperation: or, The President's Only Daughter: A Romance of Reality.* That was one beloved by the ladies. Then came my pirate adventure novels *The Black Avenger of the Spanish Main; A Thrilling Tale of Buccaneer Times*, followed by *The Red Avenger; or The Pirate King of the Floridas.*"

Ned tapped the ashes from his pipe over the side of the boat and proceeded to stuff tobacco into the bowl from his oilskin pouch. "You may have noticed that old Sam Clemens, or Mark Twain, as he likes to be known in his novel *The Adventures of Tom Sawyer* has his young hero dreaming of doing heroic things and imagining people whispering upon seeing him, that: 'It's Tom Sawyer the Pirate!—the Black Avenger of the Spanish Main.' Clearly, Twain understood that youngsters loved my books."

Fred nodded enthusiastically. "I noticed that straight away, Colonel. It is exactly as I told you, your writing has been so influential. Even on our greatest writers."

Ned struck a light and puffed on his pipe. "Well, influential or not, these humble little dime novels were not what I wanted to write. I had a burning need to write something altogether more substantial. So I embarked on my magnum opus, *The Mysteries and Miseries of New York: A Story of Real Life*. I wrote five volumes and I dedicated it to the clergy of the city of New York to highlight the plight of the poor and the destitute as well as the spread of vice and crime."

He inspected the backs of his hands and bent his fingers to peruse his nails. "It had three main plots going on in parallel, which made it quite complex. I needed a publisher to take it on, but I knew it would be a huge investment. As a teaser I published a small run of the first volume myself for twenty-five cents a copy. It sold like hot cakes, which was fortunate, as I couldn't at the time afford to print volume two. Yet my bait had worked and Berford & Company bought it and published it. Before long it had sold a hundred thousand copies, before it was sold in Britain, France and Denmark. As a result of that, all of my nautical yarns were reprinted and Ned Buntline went from being just well known around a few towns, to being a household name across America."

The moon had appeared and cast an eerie shimmering light on the Hudson.

"As you will know if you have read *The Mysteries and Miseries of New York*, that I give gamblers and bunco steerers short shrift. I spent countless hours researching the seamier side of life in New York in order to do it. I rubbed shoulders with gangsters, crooks, brothel keepers and saloon owners. I frequented the gaming houses and the parlors of the rich and famous, nosing out the depravity that lurked beneath. In my books I showed all the corruption, hypocrisy and downright dishonesty of the so-called gentlemen who ran the city. I did it by wrapping the message all up in high drama, so that the result was a series of thrilling stories that held within them good morals and a message that you can fight adversity and good will triumph over evil. It all was so popular, just the sort of things the good people of America wanted to hear. They liked the fact that there was someone prepared to write about poverty and crime and they liked and admired the streak of patriotism in my heroes and heroines. Without realizing it at the time, I had discovered the magic formula I needed for the newspaper that I was burning to start."

"You mean you had found the thing that you were going to crusade about?"

"That's right, Fred. Above all it would have a good, firm moral stance, as my readers would expect from all of my stories and novels. It would also be fiercely patriotic. When I finally started *Ned Buntline's Own*, each issue of which had a picture of myself with an idealized Old Glory banner behind the title, I promised that the reader could be assured that they were going to find out about corruption in Gotham City. Crooked gamblers would be named and shamed. Philanderers would be exposed. Clergy who led secret lives and who caroused could expect to be uncovered. The first issue rolled off the printing press on July 22, 1848. It came out weekly and sold for six cents a copy, or three dollars a year subscription."

"And the world knows how successful it was," said Fred, warming to Ned's enthusiasm for his brainchild.

"I became rich, Fred." He held a hand out to indicate the vessel they were drinking beer on. "*The Captain's Pig* is a delightful little cruiser and I love it dearly, but it was not my first boat on the Hudson. I had a yacht built and I hired a crew of eight to sail it, which will give you an idea of its size. I called it *Ned Buntline's Own*."

Suddenly, his face clouded. "Therein lies part of the sorry tale, Fred. But again, I get a little ahead of myself. The truth is that any crusading newsman is going to make enemies. I made lots. My newspaper was responsible for businesses going bust, unscrupulous employers being taken to court and for sweat shops being closed down. I received weekly death threats, the odd cobblestone was tossed through my office windows and on several occasions I was struck. I responded to everything either through the due process of the law, or with good old-fashioned law of the fist. Two people challenged me to a duel, only to withdraw the challenges when it was pointed out to them by their seconds that I had fought duels in my navy days and a fatal one in Nashville only a couple of years before."

Fred nodded. "I have news cuttings from *Knickerbocker* and from your own account in *Ned Buntline's Own*."

Ned gave a hollow, mirthless laugh. "That incident was the cause of one of the greatest miscarriages of justice against me, Fred." His hand went unconsciously to his throat, which he rubbed. "A mob almost lynched me."

Fred lay down his beer, as if it had suddenly turned bitter and he had lost the taste for it. "I also have a copy of the next issue of *Knickerbocker*, in which they rebutted the rumor that you had died."

Ned nodded and tamped down the ash on his pipe. "I wrote the letter that they quoted after reading the first account of the heinous act. Yet let us not dwell on that. Suffice to say that my reputation as a man not to be messed with, assuredly acted as a deterrent to many."

He pointed to another medal on his left lapel, beside the *Grand Order of the L. N. Fowler Society of Daughters of Temperance*. "This medal was given to me for my services to the Native American Party for my influential writing. You see, I not only had to fight injustice, but I had to rehabilitate the reputation of the Native American Party, which had suffered considerably in New York because of a man called Bill Poole, or Bill the Butcher as he was known. He was a founding member of the Bowery Boys, one of the gangs of New York. They wandered around in their stovepipe hats, smoking churchwarden pipes, spreading mayhem and justifying everything by claiming that they were patriots working for the Party. Bill the Butcher was basically a criminal that I came up against several times. In our last confrontation I outdrew him, relieved him of his pistol and very publically told him that if we ever met again I would not be so merciful. A typical bully boy, he backed down and kept out of my way ever after. Yet the damage he did to us was considerable and in my newspaper I managed to distance the American Party from him entirely. As you may know, he was shot by a rival gangster in 1855."

He went on nonchalantly, pointing to the next medal. "And this one was from the Patriotic Order of the Sons of America, another organization that I helped set up in Philadelphia in 1847. They honored me for my oratory skills."

Fred whistled. "You have had a great deal of honors bestowed, Colonel. I must make a list of them all."

Ned guffawed. "Well, one that you won't find is one from the Tammany Hall. If they had their way the only things they would have given me was a bullet or a knife in the back and a handful of dirt upon my coffin. I spent a good deal of my time writing articles in *Ned Buntline's Own* exposing their corruption. They were supposed to be a bona fide political party, but in truth they were an elite group of bankers and businessmen with foreign interests who welcomed the hundreds of thousands of British, Irish and German immigrants and organized them into a political force. They were almost entirely Catholics."

A breeze had suddenly picked up strength and blew clouds so that the moon's light dimmed as it tried to shine through the ever thickening veil of clouds.

Fred pulled the collar of his coat up and shivered slightly. "Did their religion bother you, Colonel?"

"Not at all, for a man's belief is a matter between him and God. It was the fact that the immigrants were taking our jobs, our rights. And they didn't respect our country. Even the great English writer Charles Dickens took our American hospitality and threw it back in our face. He came on a lecture tour in 1842 and wrote a travelogue that he published as *American Notes for General Circulation*. He criticized us, mainly over the use of slavery, which of course he was right to do so. As I have told you before, I had been in favor of the abolition of slavery all my life, and during the war I was prepared to fight to my dying breath to end that abominable practice. But Dickens criticized our constitution and our right to bear arms. He said it was a license for violence, where any American could shoot or knife any other American. He thought Americans serious, puritanical and lacking in humor. And as if that wasn't bad enough, he said we had poor standards of cleanliness and we all spat too much. He didn't think too highly of our spittoons."

With a look of disgust he hawked and spat over the side of the boat.

"That's what I think of fine and dandy Mister Charles Dickens and that ridiculous beard of his.

To use the expression of that character of his in *A Christmas Carol*—bah humbug!"

Suddenly, there was a boom of thunder and a crack of lightning that lit up the sky. Then the rain pelted down and they scuttled for the shelter of the cabin, their clothes already damp.

"You see, Fred!" Ned yelled as the rain beat down. "No one is allowed to criticize the old literary giant Charles Dickens even when he's dead. I say again, bah humbug!"

NOTEBOOK 6
Property of Fred E. Pond
Private & Confidential

JOTTINGS ON THE LIFE OF NED BUNTLINE
April 1881

Note 142
Colonel Judson has had many enthusiastic supporters and admirers of his works, like the newspaper *The Spirit of the Times*. (Need to look back over some issues). Yet he also had his detractors and worse, downright enemies. *The Pennsylvanian*, for example seemed especially vociferous in printing uncomplimentary accounts from other papers back in the West.

Chapter 9

FROM BLACKWELL'S ISLAND TO MAINE

Ensconced in the cabin, safe from the torrential rain that had come from nowhere and which was lashing the roof, Ned produced a flask of corn mash whiskey and two glasses.

"I'm not sure that I should," said Fred, uncertainly. "After last night—"

But Ned waved him down. "We'll have a little of this for medicinal value," he said with a grin. "I'm not going to risk either of us catching a chill. Drink it slow, that's the way."

He poured them a couple of fingers each. "Of course," he went on, "Tammany Hall was in love with foreigners and did the best they could to promote every foreign writer, artist or actor that blessed us with their presence. It galled me when foreigners were feted more than our own talented folk."

Fred noted the pinpoints of color on Ned's cheeks and from the timbre of his voice could see how passionately he felt.

"For three years since 1846 there had been a feud going on both sides of the Atlantic between the two greatest tragedian actors of our time.

There was the Irish actor William Macready and our own Edwin Forrest. Both were very fine performers, mark my words, for I had seen them both at separate times. Macready had toured America in 1844 and I saw him then. Edwin Forrest, of course, I had seen regularly over the years and had spoken with him at fashionable literary soirees. When Macready announced his second tour of America Tammany Hall, the so-called theatrical elite started extolling his genius."

"I understand that both actors were said to have hired men to sabotage the other's performances," Fred interjected.

Ned harrumphed. "Perhaps there was a little of that. However, when I wrote some pieces in *Ned Buntline's Own* I was attacked in other newspapers and my office door was beaten down. My printers were afraid for their lives and if I had not been there with my trusty Blunderbus dragoon pistol that I had used in the first year of the Mexican War—well it might have been a nasty affair.

"On May 9, 1849, the date is emblazoned on my memory for all time, a group of the Bowery Boys ruined Macready's performance of Macbeth at the Astor Place Opera House. They threw chairs and rotten eggs and vegetables at him. He wasn't actually hurt, but Tammany Hall and their pet newspapers created a mountain out of the molehill and it led to a series of public disputes. I of course was asked to address a crowd, which I did peaceably and responsibly. What happened afterwards I can't truly say, for I was not involved.

"One evening Macready was due to play again, but the Bowery Boys whipped up supporters and the theater was pelted with cobblestones. The police tried to arrest the ringleaders, but were quickly outnumbered. Then the militia was called out and the shooting began. Sadly, thirty-four citizens of New York were killed and almost one hundred and fifty were seriously wounded."

"That was terrible, Colonel," said Fred Pond, taking a large swig of whiskey.

Ned gulped his down and swiftly topped up both glasses. "Worse was to come, Fred. Because I had not been in my office but had been abroad in the streets the Tammany Hall brigade rustled up so-called eyewitnesses to say that I had been seen rousing the mob and inciting them to violence. I was arrested and thrown in jail. There I was left to languish for fifteen hours without a hearing. However, from my cell I wrote an editorial and managed to get it to my office where it was published in a special issue of *Ned Buntline's Own*. Because of that, I was released under bond and immediately boarded my yacht, mustered my eight man crew and sailed out into the Hudson Bay and then enjoyed a few days free from care, sailing along the Jersey coast. However, when I returned I was arrested again on more trumped up charges. The newspapers by this time were calling it the Astor Place Riot."

Fred sucked his teeth and then drained his whiskey. "Scurrilous, Colonel."

"Indeed! It was not until September that the trial took place, but over that time Tammany Hall had my paper closed down, because I had been betrayed by my sub-editor, who set out a grievance against me. Then at the trial they wheeled out all manner of rascals who told lies. There was not a whit of actual evidence, it was mere hearsay. It was a travesty. Judge Charles P. Daly, who was clearly in their pocket, oversaw the jury and when they found me guilty he sentenced me to one year of hard labor on Blackwell's Island."

Fred shook his head. "What a terrible miscarriage of justice. Hard labor and without a shred of tangible evidence?"

"It was, Fred, but I had lived a strenuous life and the punishment was something I took in my stride. Far worse was the closure of *Ned Buntline's Own* and the impounding of my yacht. My income was gone and creditors came out of the woodwork demanding payment. I asked that I be allowed to run my newspaper from the jail, but it was refused as was paper and ink, in case I somehow managed to get articles out to be published in any of the papers that were loyal to me. Tammany Hall had won and they were determined that I should suffer. Their tame press vilified and tried to humiliate me at every opportunity. They made much of the fact that instead of fine clothes I was forced to dress in a striped prison uniform."

"Being without the means to write must have been purgatory," said Fred, sipping his whiskey.

"It was hell, but I have been fortunate to have been blessed with not only a phenomenal imagination, but a prodigious memory. As I lay in my cell in the darkness I composed a novel. Later, when a couple of my jailors who happened to be admirers of my work began supplying me with paper and pencils I was able to transcribe the novel."

Fred began to hiccup, a fact that caused him much amusement. "Excuse—hic—me, Colonel. I—hic—seem to have hic-cups. Did you—hic—manage to publish it?"

"You hic away, good Fred. And the answer is in the affirmative, but not until I was released. On September 30, 1850 a crowd awaited the prison boat from Blackwell's Island and when the gangplank was lowered onto the docks and I stepped ashore, a free man again, they set off a cannon. A sumptuous barouche drawn by six white horses took me off to be wined and dined, while a band played 'Hail to the Chief.' "

"And—hic—the novel?"

"I called it *The Convict's Return or Innocence Vindicated*." It was published to enormous acclaim. I then re-opened *Ned Buntline's Own* and was soon back at work as if I had never been gone. People queued up in the streets for the latest issue and we had to hire an army of newsboys to meet the demand. The public had clearly missed my writings."

Ned swigged his whiskey and immediately topped up both glasses again. "I threw myself into journalism, determined to impress the public of my innocence and the iniquity of the corrupt and incompetent judicial system. I savaged Judge Daly in my newspaper columns and virtually tore his reputation to tatters."

Fred raised his glass and drank half. He waited a moment and then smiled when the half-expected hiccup did not come. "He deserved no less."

"That he did. But to tell you the truth, Fred, I grew weary of New York and I looked for other cities to ply my writing craft, even though my income was building again, so I really had no need to move. Yet there is more to life than mere money. I was restless after incarceration, Fred, so I moved to Cincinnati, which suited me for a while, but still I hankered after kindred spirits. I wanted to be with hunting men, but I also wanted to go somewhere in the heart of America to begin a campaign on behalf of the American Party. St. Louis seemed to offer all that. It was a city that attracted all of the trade from the Great Lakes and New Orleans. I had heard that fifty steamships a day would be moored in the St. Louis levee, being loaded or unloaded. Apart from that it was the terminus for the overland routes from the west. The Santa Fe trail and the Rocky Mountain fur trade brought fortunes teaming into the city each year. It called out opportunity to me.

"So there I went and set up a new magazine, *Ned Buntline's Novelist* and it immediately started to outsell every other magazine. As with my other literary ventures I used it for public good and to highlight areas where Americans were getting a raw deal. In 1854 during a local election campaign there was a riot and a fire broke out and the fire brigade were called, but things got out of hand and a young fireman, Joseph Stephens, was shot. I reported his funeral in my magazine and somehow tongues wagged and my rival newspapermen claimed that I had been the organizer of a riot."

He shook his head in amazement. "I was arrested, Fred."

"Another miscarriage of justice, Colonel!"

"Well, this time the date for the trial kept being postponed until I frankly lost patience. I had other important things to do, so I left town. You see, the Party wanted me to give lectures all over the country. I was asked to give a talk in Portland, Maine, so off I went.

"The meeting was held by the Presumpscot riverfront and a huge crowd came to hear me speak. I was talking about immigration and as I usually do I combined it with an impromptu speech on temperance. It was going well until some drunks took exception to my message. Worse, a drunken Irishman, a veritable Goliath of a man, clutching a bottle of whiskey or rum in one hand and an axe-helve in his other started to harangue me. He was soon followed by the other drunks. As usual I was more than a match for a drunken heckler, which caused much amusement in the crowd, but only increased the Irishman's ire. He mounted the dais, waving his bottle and axe-helve threateningly at me."

Ned set down his glass on the cabin floor and mimicked the Irishman. " 'What right do you have to come here, telling us that we shouldn't be here, you damned heathen.' "

Then he became himself: "I am here by right of being a native born American, sir. I am no heathen, but a good God-fearing man. But what about you, have you been naturalized?"

Ned adopted a belligerent pose. " 'Aye, to be sure I've been naturalized.' "

Then calmly, as himself again: "Well, I don't believe you have been baptized. In the name of the stars and stripes, take water."

He suddenly dashed out a hand as if to catch the imaginary Irish Goliath by the scruff of the neck and tugged and threw his imagined adversary. "I tossed him straight into the Presumpscot River."

"I was dusting my hands together as the crowd started to cheer and laugh. Then I heard a gurgling scream from the river. From the crowd one of the less-drunken friends cried out: 'He can't swim!' "

Continuing his performance Ned pulled off his coat and then reached for his boots, for he was now in full thespian swing. "I wasted no time, Fred. As quick as I could I cast off my boots—any seagoing man will tell you the same, don't risk swimming with boots on— and dived in after him. The current had already carried him some way and he was going down for a second or third time when I reached him. He was panicking and I had to knock him out and swim back against the current to get him to safety. Ropes were thrown and I tied one around him so he could be dragged back on dry land."

" 'What's your name?' I asked him as he came round upon the platform.

" 'Daniel Murphy, sor,' he says back, as he staggered to his feet. 'You saved my life, sure you did.' "

"I stood there, dripping wet and held out my

hand. 'Well let this be a lesson Daniel Murphy. Cast aside the demon drink and tell your friends to do so too. Take the pledge of sobriety and thank the Lord for letting you see tomorrow in this great land of America. Oh yes, and one of the first things I'd do is learn to swim.' "

Fred Pond slapped his knee. "I wish I had been there, Colonel."

"I wish you had, too. The effect of my life-saving act, which any Christian man would do, was remarkable. Daniel Murphy and every one of his drinking cronies took the pledge that day. News of it was reported in the *Kennebec Journal* and picked up by every single Maine newspaper. It was undoubtedly the incident that sparked the enthusiasm for temperance across the whole state of Maine. A month later Maine led the nation in passing the first state law prohibiting alcohol, except for medicinal, mechanical or manufacturing purposes. As I'm sure you know, the so-called Maine Law spread across the land and eighteen states followed."

Ned picked up his glass, drained it and held it out for a grinning, ebullient Fred Pond to fill up again.

"I'll drink to that, Colonel."

They clinked glasses and drained them.

Then Fred Pond, grinning from ear to ear, slumped sideward onto his berth. Soon he was snoring peacefully.

Ned grinned. "Young Fred can't hold his liquor." Then he fell back, slid off his berth to roll onto the cabin floor, where he remained all night as the rain beat down on the roof.

NOTEBOOK 6
Property of Fred E. Pond
Private & Confidential

JOTTINGS ON THE LIFE OF NED BUNTLINE
April 1881

Note 161
Colonel Judson has not always been consistent in his anecdotes about his wounds and scars. He has on at least five occasions shown me scars that have at times been knife, arrow or gunshot wounds. Probably best to gloss over this, lest it be thought that he overuses his prodigious literary imagination to make things up.

Chapter 10

FAMILY MAN

Ned had one of his Buntline Man O'War concoctions waiting for Fred Pond when he awoke at around ten o'clock in the morning. The cabin had been cleaned and a fresh breeze was coming through the opened door. It smelled good after the rain of the night. Ned looked spruce and bright-eyed, as if he had not imbibed at all the night before.

"I am in a world of pain, Colonel," said Fred, accepting the drink and quickly swallowing it. He belched as it hit his stomach.

"That is good, Fred. All part of my plan to show you the evils of strong drink. I am guessing that you would be willing to sign the pledge this very morning."

Fred groaned. "Give me the paper and I'll sign it right now, Colonel. I promise I will never over-indulge again."

Ned grinned. "Remember what I said, Fred. I signed it with the L. N. Fowler Society of Daughters of Temperance, but I kept my fingers crossed."

Fred nodded as he rubbed his eyes. "Um, yes. You said that because you crossed your fingers, you weren't telling a lie."

"Exactly, my boy. And if you figuratively sign the pledge, but cross your fingers you'll be able to do just what I do. That is, you'll be able to teach people the evils of drinking, but you'll still be able to remind yourself of why it is a good thing to abstain."

"I . . . I guess so Colonel."

Ned laughed. "I'll make a temperance lecturer out of you yet, Fred. You don't really need to sign the pledge, just accept that you are a strong enough man who could sign it any time you wanted to—with your fingers crossed." He slapped his knee. "But right now I'm going to cook you a hearty breakfast of bacon, eggs, and good old sourdough biscuits. That's just what your stomach needs right now."

To his surprise, Fred rather felt the need of food. Once again, the Buntline Man O'War seemed to be doing its job.

"Nothing is too good for my protégé," said Ned, opening the stove plate and heating the frying pan. "Then we'll make our way to Albany."

Protégé? Fred thought to himself with a smile. He liked the idea of being promoted from mere biographer to protégé. For some reason he felt ridiculously proud.

All day they took turns sailing, while the other wrote.

"That's the spirit, Fred. Write whenever you

have a spare moment. Never be without writing materials, those have been my guiding principles in life and I am pleased to see that you, my protégé do exactly the same."

It was the second time that Ned had used the term and it felt good to Fred Pond.

"Why did you call me your protégé, Colonel?" he ventured.

Ned sighed. "Forgive me if I presume too much, good Fred. It is just that I see much of myself in you. Like me you have a facility with words and a burning desire for exactitude, for the truth."

Fred beamed. "I do, sir. And I have to admit that I use the pen name of Will Wildwood precisely because you have used so many nom de plumes. If Mark Twain is good enough for Samuel L. Clemens and Ned Buntline for Colonel Edward Z. Judson, then Will Wildwood is good enough for me."

Ned clapped his hands. "It is a fine sobriquet, Fred. I thought so from the first moment you sent me your books. Why surely, I thought, here is a man of the same spirit as myself. Let us see what he is made of and how we get on."

Fred raised his hands emphatically. "Colonel Judson, sir. You overestimate me in so many ways. I have a liking for outdoor sports, but they are merely fishing and game shooting. I do not have your adventurous nature or your gallant heart. Where you are a writer of note and undoubted significance, I am a mere plodder, a hack."

"Not another word," Ned said firmly. "Do not deprecate yourself. Whether you have ridden with Buffalo Bill, shot with Custer or traded insults with Wild Bill Hickok, none of those things matter. It is what goes on in here that counts," he said, tapping his head.

"And what you feel in here," he added, patting his heart. "You are a writer, Fred and one whom I would be happy to hand my humble mantle onto when the time comes for me to part this earth. In the meanwhile, I am more than happy to be your guide as you write this biographical work."

Fred felt himself blush. "In that case, Colonel, I'll do my best to try and live up to your kind gesture. I'm going to make this the best darned biography ever written—apart from all of your own, that is."

Ned guffawed as he adjusted the mainsheet as they were sailing close-hauled.

"So," he said once he was satisfied. "We'll be coming into Albany soon. Have you thought of your third question for the Genie of the Hudson?"

Fred had been making another sketch, but at the question he turned the page and flattened it out ready to make notes. "As a matter of fact I have, Colonel."

"Out with it then. I will answer with the utmost honesty."

"Have you been married before?"

Ned cleared his throat. It was a question he had expected. "I have been married six times, Fred. I will list my wives precisely, but first let me ask you a question of my own. It is important, you see."

Fred gulped. "Six times?"

"I said, let me ask a question first," Ned persisted.

"Of course. Please ask anything, Colonel."

"Have you a girl yourself, Fred?"

Once again Fred Pond felt the color rise in his cheeks and he felt a slight flutter in his chest. "As a matter of fact I have, Colonel. She is the dearest, sweetest creature imaginable."

Then his face clouded slightly and his eyes fell to look at his hands, which he had bunched into fists. "But she is an heiress to a railroad magnate and there is no question of me courting her. We . . . We exchange poetry by post."

Ned held up a hand. "Ah, there you are admitting to a self-imposed stumbling block straight away. You are putting yourself in a position of disadvantage because you perceive that she is from higher up the social ladder than yourself."

"Her father is wealthy beyond belief, Colonel. I am but an impecunious—"

"No, no, no! You do it again. A writer must hold his or her head high, for you are following a noble profession in letters. You are a creative, sir. A scribbler rather than a mere scrabbler after mammon! You use your brain for loftier things than the accumulation of wealth."

Suddenly he reached a hand into his pocket and came out with a handful of coins, which he flung over the side of *The Captain's Pig*. As they splashed into the water he turned triumphantly.

"Look what I did. I gave my money away. But what use is money to fish? What use have animals for it? Do birds buy food with money? No, Fred, money is not real. Dollar bills or coins, they are nothing really. Money is merely a symbol. A wealthy man simply has more of these symbols than a beggar. Yet a beggar can think the richest thoughts. He can be a wiser man than the rich man in his mansion. So, let this be your lesson, don't compare yourself with another person using money as the measuring stick."

Fred laughed heartily and plunged a hand into his own pocket to cast more coins into the Hudson. "What a wonderful release, Colonel. You are right, of course."

Ned nodded. "It is a lesson I learned early in life, when I was but seventeen years old. It was when I was still in the navy and we sailed into Havana. I had several days off as it was the Shrovetide carnival season. And what a sight it was. Everyone was dressed up in glittering, sumptuous costumes. There were parades, wine in abundance and dancing. As young naval officers I and my comrades found ourselves much in demand. We were invited to taverns, theaters and masked balls.

"At one such affair I met Seberina Escudero, the daughter of the Conte and Contessa Escudero de San Juan de Jaruco. Since I was fluent in Spanish, unlike my other officer friends, I was able to socialize with abandon. Her parents were Cuban nobility and fabulously wealthy. They were more than happy for me to dance with their beautiful daughter. Seberina was the same age as myself and we fell in love that very night under the stars of the Caribbean sky."

Fred noted a mistiness had come over Ned's eyes and had no doubt that at that moment he was reliving his early romantic encounter.

"I visited several times over the time of my leave and the Conte and his wife took to me, thanks to my ability to tell them tales of adventure, my skill at chess and my knowledge of the great Spanish writers. Seberina and I held hands, kissed and told each other our deepest secrets and desires."

Ned sighed and clutched the tiller. "I did not want to leave, but leave I had to. But not before Seberina and I secretly plighted our troth. We wrote whenever we could, which is not easy when you are sailing the seas and don't touch land very often. I always had her address and could reach her, but I could not tell her my destination, thanks to the secrecy of the navy and the Seminole War, which I told you about previously.

"Well, when the war was over and I did eventually receive a letter from her it made my heart sink, for her parents had arranged for her to marry a Cuban nobleman. That was when I cast everything to the wind, Fred. I resigned my commission forthwith. I threw away money, status and the prospect of a glittering naval career."

"Goodness, but I thought that you immediately went to work for the Northwest Fur Company?"

Ned hesitated for but a moment. "No, Fred. I did work for them, but that was a little over a year later. First I made my way to Cuba aboard a schooner. There, upon the wedding eve I climbed over the boundary walls of the Escudero estate, silenced the guard dogs with an old Indian trick I had learned and climbed up to Seberina's room. She would have been marrying into great wealth, but she was mine and I was hers, so we eloped right there and then. We were married by an old priest that very night, before making off to sea."

"I don't know what to say, Colonel. How romantic."

"It was romantic and we were happy for a whole year. When she died of yellow fever I was heartbroken and needed to get away from this cruel world. That was when I went fur hunting."

Fred gasped. "How tragic! I am so sorry, Colonel. I did not know."

Ned's eyes glistened and a tear rolled down his cheek. "Such is life, Fred. We must all move on from tragedy. Just as I have moved on from my most recent tragedy, when little Irene was taken from us earlier this year."

"That must have been the bitterest of blows, Colonel."

The writer nodded emphatically and, producing a handkerchief, blew his nose loudly. "Losing a child is the worst thing that can happen to anyone. To a man such as I, who loves his children," he said, patting the back of his head, "I have a well-developed philoprogenitiveness faculty, as the phrenologist Doctor Spurzheim told my father when I was a boy—it is purgatory. It is another example of how I have suffered, Fred."

"You have lost other children?" Fred asked, his face registering sorrow for Ned.

"Not from the Grim Reaper, yet lose children I have. I married a second time in 1848 when I returned to New York. A friend of mine, Lieutenant Ralph Porter introduced me to a young lady, Annie Abigail Bennett who was one of New York's social elite. Her parents had come from Britain when she was a child of five years of age and they had prospered. Annie and I hit it off immediately and her parents approved of me, for I was already well known as a novelist and the owner of *Ned Buntline's Own*. After a whirlwind romance we were married in Trinity Church.

"Well, I moved in with the family, despite my wariness of the British. We had a daughter, little Mary, who was the apple of my eye. Unfortunately, it was at the time of the Astor Place fiasco, which as I told you, resulted in my wrongful imprisonment, the loss of my yacht and financial ruin. Annie's parents persuaded her that she should divorce me, which she did. She took my little Mary and I have barely seen her these past thirty odd years. I lost her, damn Annie's British parents' small-mindedness."

Fred noted the writer's raised voice, but said nothing. Instead, he jotted a note about Ned's antipathy against the British.

"I remained a single man for several years then, Fred," Ned went on.

He smiled to himself as his mind flashed before him the many mistresses that he had lived with or kept houses for over the years. He decided to say nothing to Fred of them for it would take too long. Besides, they were not married to him, so in his mind they did not count.

"Then in 1857 I had relocated to The Eagle's Nest in the Adirondacks. That was the first Eagle's Nest, not the one you know at Stamford. I was enjoying my freedom and spent my time hunting, shooting and fishing. Chauncey Hathorn, the son of a state senator had a resort at Saratoga. He took a hunting party up to Blue Mountain Lake and persuaded me to take some of these city types fishing. When he took them to meet me at my house he was shocked at the state of my bachelor home. He persuaded me to take on a housekeeper and he said he knew just the person."

Ned sighed. "A lovely woman was Eva Marie Gardiner, although not perhaps as beautiful as Annie or Seberina, yet she had charm by the bucketful. She was a lot younger than me, of course. I was thirty-four and she but eighteen, but it was not long before we fell deeply in love. Within a month we had married and were so looking forward to building a family together. But it wasn't to be. She died when she was lying in after the birth of our daughter and so did little Nellie."

The handkerchief was produced again and Fred respectfully remained silent while Ned blew his nose and shed some more tears.

Ned had handed over the tiller to Fred while he went into the cabin to fortify himself. He returned with a bottle and two glasses.

"I don't think I should drink, Colonel," Fred protested. "There is a lot of traffic on the Hudson right now." He pointed to a steamer going in the other direction. As if on cue it sounded its steam whistle and inevitably the usual waves and calls rang out from passengers alerted to *The Captain's Pig* with the famous Ned Buntline aboard. Ned and Fred acknowledged them all with forced laughs and waves of bonhomie.

"Nonsense, Fred. This is for medicinal purposes, for your question, so rightly put to me, has opened up some old wounds that are deeper than those caused by mere bullets and arrows. You must drink with me."

With a reluctant smile Fred accepted the glass, determined in himself to toss its contents overboard at the first opportunity.

"Now where was I," said Ned, after draining his glass and wiping his mouth with the back of his sleeve. "Ah yes, number four!" He poured a finger of whiskey and quickly drained it, as if in need of feeling the solace the liquor could give.

"Kate Myers and I were married in Sing Sing by the chaplain on November 2, 1860. I took her to the Eagle's Nest in the Adirondacks and we spent the first winter snowed in. I wrote umpteen novels and she kept talking of escaping back to civilization, but since I stole and hid her shoes she had no choice but to stay."

"Did you have children with her, Colonel?"

"We had four. Mary Carrolita born in 1862 afore I went to war. She was born in the Eagle's Nest. Irene Elizabeth was born in 1863 in

Chappaqua, New York. Alexander in 1865 in Valhalla and Edwardina in Chappaqua in 1867. I loved them all, its just a shame that Kate proved to be so possessive."

"She wanted all your attention, Colonel?" Fred asked.

Ned nodded as he poured a good slug of whiskey and knocked it back. "Drink up, my boy," he said, spying Fred raising his glass in preparation to toss the contents over the side.

Fred nodded quickly and downed his glass.

"Have another," said Ned, reaching over and topping the glass up. "Yes, but when I just couldn't give her everything, she divorced me in 1871 and actually did take everything. All my sweet children and a great deal of money. I was distraught, Fred, so I demolished the Eagle's Nest and moved to Stamford where I built the home where I now live."

"And so you married Anna?"

Ned shook his head. "Not then. Before that I married my fifth wife, Lovanche Swart. Now whereas Kate had been possessive, Lovanche should have been a prison turnkey. She never wanted to let me out of her sight. Fortunately, I managed to get a divorce from her before I met Anna."

Fred did not see that Ned had crossed fingers behind his back, for things had not been quite as he had told them. The truth was that he had married Lovanche in 1864 while he was on a furlough from the army, and so had been married to both women and led a contented double family life right up until 1871 when he met Anna and had been exposed in the newspapers as a bigamist. Kate had been incensed and divorced him, while Lovanche had agreed to accept fifty dollars a month in exchange for signing a stipulation not to disturb, trouble or annoy him or anyone connected with him so long as he kept up payments.

"So I married Anna Fuller on October 3, 1871 in Stamford and we have lived happily in the Eagle's Nest ever since." He eyed Fred's glass. "Drink up, my boy."

Fred shook his head and placed the glass on the deck. "Actually, Colonel, I think I'd better concentrate. That is the Albany Basin up ahead, unless I am mistaken. It's getting mighty busy and I can already feel the whiskey going to my head."

Ned stared at him with glassy eyes. "Quite so. Good man. Look, I think I'll just lie in the cabin while you take *The Captain's Pig* in and moor up. I have a little writing to finish."

Moments later Fred could hear the sound of Ned scribbling away. Then he put his mind to the business of sailing into the harbor and finding a mooring amid the hundreds of canal boats and the fifty odd steamboats.

"Colonel, we're here," he called above all the noise of the harbor when all was done. "I have one question that is niggling at me. It is not a new one, it is to do with the last question."

Ned emerged unsteadily from the cabin with a hearty grin. "What niggles, good Fred?"

"You said you had been married six times and you have accounted for six wives. Yet you said that you were married to Daisy Blanche Buntline, too. That makes seven, surely."

Ned was looking past him and his face suddenly went serious. "It looks as if you are about to get your answer, my boy."

There was the ratcheting sound of a gun hammer being pulled back and Fred slowly turned round.

Standing on the quay, dressed in men's range clothes rather than widow's weeds was Daisy Blanche Buntline.

"Get your sorry butt up here, Ned Buntline," she snapped, the gun steady and pointing unwaveringly at Ned's chest. "I want what's mine—husband!"

Chapter 11

THE SHARPSHOOTING ANGEL

Fred Pond immediately jumped in front of Ned with his arms outstretched. "Don't shoot the colonel!" he cried. "He . . . he's not well and you already wounded him." He looked over his shoulder at the astonished Ned.

"Twice," he added. "You near as hell blew his earlobes off. I won't let you hurt him again."

Daisy Blanche Buntline's jaw tightened and she frowned as she eyed Fred with surprise. "Oh, you won't, will you?" she replied.

"No, ma'am. I am Will Wildwood and I . . . I am the colonel's biographer!"

"His biographer? You are Ned Buntline's biographer?" she said in a mocking tone.

Fred puffed his lean chest up proudly. "I am so!" He stared defiantly at her. Then he realized just how attractive the woman was. She was around forty years old he guessed, with a good figure, a pretty face with full red lips and tumbling red hair under a wide-brimmed Stetson.

From behind him Ned called out: "Will Wildwood here is my protégé, ma'am. He's a fine writer and a good man."

"So, you're hiding behind him now, are you,

you low down, good for nothing hustler!" she snapped.

"Ha! And you lost the two grizzly bears that were guarding you in Stamford, I see," Ned said.

Then suddenly Daisy Blanche's firm mouth softened and curved into a smile. Then she laughed, a wonderful, melodic sound that seemed inconsistent with her up to then aggressive demeanor. Deftly, she uncocked her weapon and stowed it in the holster at her hip.

"Of course I got rid of them," she replied. "If they couldn't take care of an old coot like you, what use were they to me." She shook her head. "You'll be the death of me one day, Ned Buntline, I do swear. So let's talk turkey. Have you got it?"

Fred was still standing in front of Ned with his arms outstretched. He suddenly felt a little foolish and lowered them to his sides.

Ned began to chuckle. "I have it in the cabin, Daisy Blanche. Just as I said I would."

Fred took a pace sideward and looked back and forth at Ned and Daisy Blanche. "I am confused here. You two have had some sort of communication?"

Ned's chuckle turned into his usual guffaw, which set Daisy Blanche off again. Despite himself Fred found their laughter infectious and started to chortle. Soon they were all three doubled up with mirth as if they had been enjoying the finest joke together.

"Yes, Fred, we've communicated."

"I think whiskey is in order," said Daisy Blanche. "It's always a fine way of getting the truth out of Ned Buntline. And the thing is, my own mouth is drier than a spadefoot toad's tongue on a hot day in the Mohave desert."

"Follow me into the cabin, then," said Ned. "It will be a tight squeeze, but I can certainly offer you the hospitality of *The Captain's Pig*."

"I'll drink to that," agreed Fred. And this time he meant it.

Sitting on the berths in the cramped cabin they clinked glasses and drank to each other's health.

"So can you explain what this is all about?" Fred asked.

"It has been an adventure and an opportunity to get to know each other better, Fred," said Ned, taking out a fresh bottle from a cabinet. "But I admit there was a little subterfuge. You remember that I told you I sent three telegrams."

"You only told me about two of them."

"Daisy Blanche received the third," Ned replied. "It simply said—"

"It said to meet in Albany Basin. I'll bring the goods," Daisy Blanche volunteered, before downing her whiskey and holding out her glass for replenishment.

Fred started to sip his whiskey, but at a disapproving scowl from Daisy Blanche he swallowed it in one gulp and with a sheepish grin held out his glass to Ned.

"Wh . . . what were the goods?" he ventured.

Ned held out the large notebook and flicked through it, showing his neat, copperplate handwriting filling each page. "My latest novel—long overdue, I admit—entitled *The Sharpshooting Angel*." He held it out to Daisy Blanche. "You can read it now, my dear, or wait until it is published and distributed to every bookstore and emporium in the land. It will make you famous beyond your wildest dreams."

Daisy Blanche took the book and started to read. "That's what you said years ago, Ned. Just before you left town in such a hurry!"

Ned gave her a crestfallen look. "I had to, Daisy Blanche. I had to evade the Pinkerton man."

He deliberately did not enlighten them why a member of the Pinkerton Agency had taken an interest in him and he had no intention of mentioning any of his former wives again.

"None of us knew where you went," continued Daisy Blanche. "You left us all there with the rent to pay to the theater and all those restaurant bills, to say nothing of the printer for all those handbills."

"I sent the money. Did you not get it from Horse Face Charlie?"

"He skedaddled like you, Ned. It's taken me all this time to track you down—husband!"

Fred was starting to feel dizzy and was having difficulty comprehending. "Could you both begin again? For a start, are you or are you not married?"

"We are!" said Daisy Blanche.

"We are not!" replied Ned.

"Are too!"

"We never . . ."

"You know we did. More times than the notches on John Wesley Hardin's guns."

Fred eyed them unsteadily. "You . . . know John Wesley Hardin?"

Daisy Blanche nodded. "We both did. We played poker with him in Pensacola, Florida just the day before he was caught on a train." She sniggered. "And big bad John is now the superintendent of the Huntsville Prison Sunday School."

Then with a coquettish lifting of an eyebrow she said challengingly to Ned: "He reckoned he had 42 notches."

Ned darted a glance at Fred, relieved to see that the significance of the notches seemed lost on his protégé.

"Now come, Daisy Blanche, you know full well that the wedding was a sham, we were married in name only. Otherwise, not really."

"Do I have to show you the certificate again?" said Daisy Blanche, with a sigh.

Ned drank his whiskey and then topped up all

three glasses. "Come on, Daisy Blanche, you know as well as I that it was simply a publicity stunt to advertise the show. The preacher was just an actor and the name on that certificate is Buntline—which is just my pen name. Legally, the marriage doesn't exist."

"That's as may be," she conceded. "But you made promises, Ned. You welched on them."

"I still—don't understand," said Fred, in confusion. "What show? Where and when?"

Ned stared at him for a moment, then nodded. "Okay, Fred. I haven't introduced you properly. Meet Daisy Blanche Buntline, actress and sharpshooter extraordinaire."

Daisy Blanche smiled at Fred and held out her hand.

"A . . . a pleasure, ma'am," said Fred reaching his hand out, then staring at her in alarm.

As if by magic, for he had not seen her hand move, her gun had appeared in her hand and the hammer was pulled back.

Daisy Blanche laughed and instantly uncocked the weapon, spun it by the trigger guard to skillfully reholster it in one move. "Sorry, Will, or Fred or whatever name you are using. It's an old habit that I can't help myself with." She patted his shoulder and bestowed a lovely smile upon him, which totally disarmed him. "I see that Ned has you hiding your identity already."

"Gosh, I've never seen anything so fast in all

my life," he enthused, like a giddy school kid. "My real name is Pond, Daisy Blanche. Fred Eugene Pond. Will Wildwood is just my pen name."

They shook hands. "He does that to all his actors and associates," she explained. "He renames us all. Look at William Frederick Cody, a perfectly respectable name, but everyone knows him as Buffalo Bill. The same with James Butler Hickok, who hated being called Wild Bill Hickok. Martha Jane Canary, though, well I guess she liked her Calamity Jane monicker, but I hear that Mary Katherine Horony isn't too happy that you called her Big Nose Kate in that magazine story about her. Her boyfriend Doc Holliday has said if he gets the opportunity he'll fix your teeth for you."

Ned refused to allow himself to imagine Calamity Jane, not when he was talking to another of his former mistresses. He waved his hand unconcernedly. "A mere literary device to enhance the tale. The reading public like names with a sparkle. Yet why should Kate worry, my story *The Hungarian Gambling Queen* made her famous. But don't worry, I shall make it all well with Doc, when next I see him."

"You do that, but just make sure that you publish this novel that you promised me three years ago," Daisy Blanche returned. "And the play you said you'd write."

"The novel is here, duly written in front of Fred Pond's own eyes. It will be in the hands of my publisher tomorrow. As for the play, I shall start upon it as soon as I return home."

The whiskey bottle did another circuit and they all tossed off their drink.

"So . . . So," began Fred, his voice starting to slur. "What's this show you were talking about?"

Ned had been stuffing tobacco into his corncob pipe. Tamping it down he struck a light and puffed thoughtfully. "It was three years ago in Florida. I was on a temperance tour and I saw Daisy Blanche in a show in a one-horse-place called Jugtown. She was quite the most talented sharpshooter I ever saw."

"It was a medicine show," Daisy Blanche explained. "My brother Nathaniel had invented the best darned cure-all that was ever sold. Professor Nathaniel Starbottle's Universal tonic it was called. Of course, he wasn't a professor at all, but he was a pretty decent druggist's clerk back in Ohio. He'd tried to become a doctor, but—well, that's a long story that you don't need to know about. The thing is, we came from an acting and acrobat family and my daddy had seen that I had a gift with guns, so he taught me how to handle them really well. Any type of gun, actually. Why I could shoot the—"

"— the wings off a horse-fly," interrupted Ned, pointing to his ears with the stem of his pipe.

"As she demonstrated in that little charade at Hamilton House in Stamford. Like I said, when she fired at me I knew I wasn't in the slightest danger. It was a show for the crowd."

"It wasn't a show at all. I was meaning business and that was to humiliate you, which it did."

Ned grunted. "Well, I telegraphed you, didn't I?"

"You did, but you denied you knew me in front of that crowd. You were saving face as usual, Ned Buntline!"

The dime novelist shrugged his shoulders. "I have my reputation to think of, Daisy Blanche. Anyway, I wrote the novel in two days, so what are you worried about?"

Fred waved his hands. "Wait a moment. Daisy Blanche was telling me about this medicine show, Colonel."

She smiled at him and continued, much to Ned's consternation. With a scowl he puffed furiously on his pipe, filling the cabin with a thick blue haze of fumes.

"Apart from me and Nathaniel there was a couple of girls that danced and juggled, a strongman called Olaf, who pretended to have been a weakling until he started on the tonic. Part of the show was for me to come on with pebble-thick spectacles and a cane to tap around as if I could hardly see. My brother would tell the crowd how a bottle of his tonic cured me, so that I could become a sharpshooting wonder. Then I'd demonstrate by shooting plates and old bottles that he'd throw in the air. He'd show them his thick hair, which he'd always had, but which he said had grown back from being as bald as a turkey vulture after he started taking his tonic."

"They were very popular with the crowd, but they needed handling right," went on Ned. "I saw Daisy Blanche's talent and offered to take them to Chicago, which I did. We had it all arranged, a theater booked, playbills printed and—we very publically got married."

"You were drunk as a skunk when we did it with my brother Nathaniel dressed up as a preacher."

Ned looked surprised. "Ah, so it was Nathaniel who did the deed?"

"See how drunk you were," Daisy Blanche said, with a hint of triumph.

"Anyway," Ned continued. "I thought that if we used the famous Ned Buntline name, it would attract a crowd. Which it seemed to do."

Daisy Blanche harrumphed. "Only it also attracted a Pinkerton detective from one of your wives! Or maybe it was just another mistress, like me. We never found out, because the next thing we knew, you had gone. We couldn't go ahead with the show, because we hadn't had time to rehearse the play, *The Sharpshooting Angel* that you were supposed to be writing around me. As well as the dime novel!"

"I think that's enough, Daisy Blanche. It wasn't a real marriage, that's all Fred needs to know."

Fred was barely taking anything in. The cabin was full of smoke and his vision was getting blurred. Now there seemed to be not one, but two Daisy Blanche women, both of them claiming to be Mrs. Ned Buntline.

"I need a drink," he said, draining his glass. As it hit his stomach he began to laugh. "I really . . . I really need to write all this down," he said. "But first I need a little air."

He stood up, forgetting that the ceiling was a mere five feet from the floor of the cabin. He felt the explosive thud on his head then all went black and he felt himself falling into a dark pool of unconsciousness.

He dimly heard Daisy Blanche's concerned voice. "Now look what you've done, Ned Buntline."

NOTEBOOK 8
Property of Fred E. Pond
Private & Confidential

JOTTINGS ON THE LIFE OF NED BUNTLINE
May 1881

Note 183
Colonel Judson has been married six times and seems to have had several lady friends. As a publicity trick he was "married" to Daisy Blanche Buntline, an actress and sharpshooter. She shot both his earlobes in Stamford. The colonel has written a dime novel for her and also plans to write a play. Both are to be called *The Sharpshooting Angel*.

Best not to mention any of this in the biographical sketches or the book.

Chapter 12

PLAINS AND PRAIRIES

It was another two weeks before Fred Pond could visit the Eagle's Nest again. By this time the first of his articles about Ned had been published in *Wildwood's Magazine*, to great popularity if not exactly critical acclaim.

Anna Judson looked just about ready to produce her baby, but kept busy as usual fussing around Ned like a mother hen. It was a situation that the great author was perfectly happy with. As he said to Fred, once they were in his inner sanctum:

"I have seen childbirth many times, my boy. It is best for a woman to be as distracted as possible before her labor. I saw Hopi squaws going about their daily chores until the moment of birth, when they would take themselves off to a quiet place and have the baby before starting their work again. I have even delivered babies myself, once when I was leading a wagon train to Oregon and another time during a lecture that I was giving on the evils of gambling. In the latter case the pregnant lady was the mistress of a professional gambler who had run out and left her high and dry. She called her son, 'Fourflush' in the hope that he would never take after his absent father."

"Do you know if he did or not?"

"I'd take bets that he became a gambler like his father. He had a diamond shaped birthmark on his right wrist, so I guess it will be taken as a sign. But the thing is that in all these cases they were busy right up until their time. Little Fourflush's mother was totally distracted by my oratory, apparently."

"You have had such a full life, Colonel. Indeed, my mailbag was full of letters after the first article was published. The commonest thing readers wanted to know is more about Buffalo Bill and Wild Bill Hickok. Your novel *Buffalo Bill, King of Border Men—The Wildest and Truest Story I Ever Wrote* has been just about one of the most widely sold books in America. You know that I've admired it and read it over a dozen times."

Ned nodded thoughtfully. "Literature is like that, Fred. One never knows when one will write the story that strikes the right note and proves more popular than its fellows. I wrote that in serial form in the *New York Weekly* for Street & Smith over three months back in 1870. Neither them nor I could have predicted just how big a deal it would be."

Fred pointed to the valise covered with travel stickers in the corner of the room. "You showed me your puppet of Buffalo Bill that first time I visited you. You said you believed that you were responsible for making him the legend that he became."

"That's true, without question, Fred. And I invented the Wild West show on the stage," Ned replied matter-of-factly.

"So how did you meet him and Wild Bill Hickok?"

Ned reached across his desk and opened a cigar box and drew out two large cigars. He tossed one to Fred and after biting its end placed one between his teeth. He slowly lit it and then threw the box of vestas to Fred. He sat back, blowing a series of perfect smoke rings.

"You see those smoke rings, Fred? Do they suggest anything to you?"

"Smoke signals, Colonel?" said Fred, between puffs.

"Exactly! It was seeing smoke signals while I was scouting in Nebraska in 1869 that alerted me that something was about to happen. I was an expert on their meaning, of course."

He savored his smoke as he allowed the pearler he had just spun to Fred time to sink in. In truth he had never seen actual smoke signals and was about as much an expert on them as he was on French haute cuisine, a subject about which he knew precisely nothing. Still, such details should never interfere with a good story, he believed.

"There had been an unpleasant skirmish at Summit Springs, where a band of Sioux and

Cheyenne renegades under Chief Tall Bull were flushed out by some of my fellow scouts. I heard all about it when I reported in to Fort McPherson. A German woman prisoner had been released and one of the scouts, Bill Cody, had tracked down and taken care of Tall Bull."

"And did you meet Bill Cody there?"

"No, I had to go tracking, because he just wanted to go off and find fresh adventures."

"Like one of King Arthur's Knights of the Round Table," Fred suggested.

"Indeed. Well, I tracked him for two days, hailed his camp in the proper, safe manner and got the whole story out of him. Back then, he was and is essentially a humble man, who has never sought publicity. When I suggested to him that I should write his story for the *New York Weekly*, I had to about twist his arm to get him to agree."

Fred had been trying unsuccessfully to blow smoke rings. He gave a soft laugh. "An incredible story, Colonel. So typical of the Buffalo Bill we all love."

Ned nodded with a grin. The truth had been quite different. The real hero had been a Major Frank North, but when Ned sought him out he was given short shrift. He was just about to catch a train back east when he saw a drunken fellow sleeping under a wagon. Some questions to loafers revealed that this young strapping man, with long hair, a goatee beard and a flamboyant broad brimmed hat was indeed a scout, although he had nothing whatever to do with the skirmish. That mattered not a whit to Ned, for he looked every bit the western hero.

Over a meal and more drinks in the nearest saloon Ned extracted William Cody's history. A deal was made and the germ of an idea for a story had started to form in Ned's mind. He had written half of it within the first four hours of his train journey back East.

"One surprising thing about the story was the way you portrayed Wild Bill Hickok as Buffalo Bill's trusty sidekick in *Buffalo Bill, the King of the Border Men*. Yet all the world knows he was his own man. A lawman of true grit."

Ned made the sign of the cross over his heart. "Rest In Peace, Wild Bill Hickok." Then: "He was indeed a man of true grit, Fred. Call my reference to him as a sidekick just a piece of poetic license. However you care to look at it, my stories made them both household names across America within mere weeks."

He blew a slow stream of smoke ceilingwards, recalling his first meeting with the famed gun-fighting lawman. It had not gone well for Ned. In fact, Ned's whole reason for visiting Fort McPherson in Nebraska, was to interview Wild Bill Hickok in order to write a popular article about him and then a dime novel.

As a character, he promised to be everything

Ned could have wished for. He saw him standing at a saloon bar, whiskey in hand. Over six feet tall, lithe, sinewy with fine, almost chiseled features and a long straggling mustache to go with long, tumbling, curly hair. He was wearing a red shirt and fancy black tie, a broad-brim hat and a well-cut frock coat. Buckskin leggings were tucked into tall boots and two ivory handled Navy Colts hung from each hip.

Adopting his usual ebullient and brash manner Ned rushed over to him, saying "There's my man. I want you."

It was not the sort of thing to say to a man who had survived several gunfights and who had lived on both sides of the law. Hickok had his whiskey halfway to his lips, but upon Ned's words he dropped the glass, drew both guns and swiveled round, all before the glass hit the floor. Seeing Ned was no real threat, he casually fired two shots into the floor in front of the dime novelist before nonchalantly blowing the smoke from the barrels of his guns. Then he demanded that Ned pay the saloon for the damage to the floor and buy him a replacement whiskey. As soon as Ned's money was on the counter he told Ned he had twenty-four hours to get out of town.

It was for this reason that Ned had relegated him in importance in the dime novel.

"A great and chivalrous man, that was Wild Bill," Ned said, almost reverently. "We always got on well. Yet the truth be known, Fred, he was remarkably shy. So was Buffalo Bill to begin with."

"No, Colonel, surely not! Both of them? I can't believe it."

"Oh both were as brave and fierce as lions, but neither was prepared for facing an audience from the stage. Yet that was what I made them do in my play and as a result of it I invented the Wild West Stage Show."

Fred lay his cigar down in an ashtray and pulled out his notebook and pencil. "Tell me, Colonel."

Ned stretched his legs out in front of him. "Well, it was two years after my dime novel had made such a hit. I had kept up a correspondence with both Buffalo Bill and Texas Jack Omohundro, another fellow scout and Indian fighter. I had suggested to them that we should indeed put on a spectacular Wild West Stage Show. They agreed to meet me in Chicago and I would put them on a real stage, not just one that they had ridden in, driven or saved from robbers."

Fred laughed at the joke and noted it all down. "Good. I like it."

"So I arrived in Chicago on the Thursday morning, and Buffalo Bill and Texas Jack arrived in the evening. They were supposed to bring twenty Indian braves for the show. Judge my consternation when they came without an Indian. What were we to do, Fred? The Amphitheater, the biggest theater in Chicago was hired for the next Monday night at a heavy cost. We had no Indians, and it was to be an Indian show. Jim Nixon the proprietor was not happy and threatened to break our contract. 'We must now have a play,' says he. 'Fear not, you shall have one!' I replied. So, I went out and hired ten actors who were waiting around for something to do, and set Bill and Jack the task of making Indians of them.

"I went upstairs to my room to write a play, which I did in four hours! I hired a gang of copyists to transcribe each page so that they all would have their lines. It was a blood-curdling and gory tragedy of the plains, entitled *The Scouts of the Plains*. Buffalo Bill was made the hero, but I was cast as Cale Durg, a rough, tough, no nonsense scout. Basically, I played myself."

He coughed modestly. "It was a fine play if I say so, although the scouts were not keen on acting. Texas Jack asked Bill how long it would take him to learn his lines. 'About six months, I calculate,' he replied. Then Texas Jack said it would take him that long to learn his first line. Yet I pushed them and encouraged them. Whiskey seemed to loosen their tongues and eased their memories.

"We had three rehearsals—one on Friday and two on Saturday. My own part was not written at all, as I merely had a cue at the end, and led up to it with any sort of talk I pleased.

"The eventful evening came on December

16, 1872. The curtain rose on an audience of perhaps three thousand. I gave a rather brilliant, free-ranging soliloquy, such as I gave you the other night under the stars, but this was entirely impromptu. It was about frontier life and roaming the plains with my old pards Buffalo Bill and Texas Jack, when, at the cue, in they stalked. The audience rose and howled a welcome to them. The cheer was prolonged and embarrassing but at last it subsided, and the time came for Buffalo Bill to speak. Only, he had forgotten his part and stood like a statue. The prompter gave him the words, but nothing would come out of his mouth, but mumbling, gurgling ahems. I told him to say something—anything. But he was speechless, Fred."

"How embarrassing for you, Colonel," returned Fred.

"I led him in. I said to him: 'Why, you've been off buffalo-hunting with Milligan, haven't you?' Fortunately, that woke him up. He looked at Milligan and his friends, whom I had invited and obtained a box for, and he told them in plain language the story of his last buffalo hunt. Then we all got warmed up, and *The Scouts of the Plains* went off in a lively manner. It was a highly successful show, which made a handsome profit for us all."

What Ned decided to omit was that they immediately traveled to St. Louis to see if they could duplicate the success before Christmas. The show opened on December 23 at DeBarr's Grand Opera House and it attracted widespread attention. Unfortunately, among those were several politicians who recalled only too clearly the St. Louis Riot of twenty years before. Before the curtain was supposed to go up on the performance Ned was arrested by Deputy County Marshal Nathan Reinstaedtler for having jumped bail before his trial in 1854. Inevitably, he was marched before Circuit Court Judge Primm who set further bail at one thousand dollars. That allowed Ned to appear as Cale Durg once again that evening, but by the next morning, he jumped bail again and he and the troupe made for Cincinatti, where they opened a re-named play, *Scouts of the Prairie* at Pike's Opera House.

"Cincinatti, where we played next, loved us all. Then we went to Albany in February and on to Boston in March. Then we went to Arch Street Theater in Philadelphia. We knocked them out, Fred. They loved us. That was where we were joined by James Butler Hickok."

"I hadn't realized that he hadn't been with you all from the start."

"Oh no. It was not until we had considerable success. Then I and Bill Cody had prevailed upon him to come and join us, for the whole of America had seen how famous I had made Buffalo Bill and Texas Jack. He agreed to come, attracted more by the lure of money than of fame, I think."

"And how did he take to acting?"

Ned screwed up his face. "Not that good, to be honest. He couldn't remember his lines and when he could he refused to use what he called 'Buntline's flowery talk.' On stage he spat out the cold tea that was given to him instead of whiskey and when he got bored he liked to liven things up by getting up close behind the actors who were dressed up as Indians and firing his gun at their legs rather than over their heads, so that they got burned. That made them dance and leap and whoop and holler, instead of just dropping dead like they were supposed to. He was encouraged by the audience response, who thought it all quite hilarious."

Fred smiled at the idea of the scene that Ned had conjured up. "He was a free spirit not used to theatricality?" he suggested.

"We all were, Fred. All of us were men of action, people who had seen battle, death at close range and who thrived on danger. Yet we were giving the gentle folk in the east a taste of life in the West. No, Wild Bill Hickok was a complex man."

"One of the bravest," said Fred Pond. "Everyone knows that."

"Indubitably. As brave as a lion, without a care for personal safety when faced by an opponent with a gun, or when going up against several outlaws by himself. It is said that he had killed upwards of a hundred bad men. Yet he was also deeply superstitious."

"In what way?"

"At meals he threw spilled salt over his left shoulder, carried a lucky rabbit's foot in his vest pocket and always spat to the right." He nodded toward the copper spittoon from Nuttall and Mann's Saloon in Deadwood. "What stories Hickok's spittoon could tell. After Wild Bill was murdered, I asked old Abner Nuttall if I could buy it to maybe write a dime novel around it. He was only too keen to get rid of it, because he and all his customers were convinced it contained bad luck, so he sent it to me as a gift. Ever since then it has been 'Hickok's spittoon' in my mind."

He sighed, as if recounting this tale brought back painful memories. "But when Wild Bill joined our troupe and we did a saloon scene he insisted that the spittoon had to be placed to his right, never his left, or he wouldn't use it. He'd just spit tobacco juice on the floor where he reckoned it should have been, whether there was an actor or actress standing there or not."

Fred clicked his tongue then looked reverently at the spittoon. "Perhaps you should write such a dime novel about it, Colonel. But what about the famous dead man's hand? Everyone knows that when he was shot by the coward Jack McColl in Deadwood he had been dealt the ace of clubs, the ace of spades, the eight of clubs, the eight of spades and the queen of hearts. Aces and eights in black."

"He wouldn't have known their significance, Fred. They were called that after he died. Whatever he'd been dealt would have been called that."

"I suppose so," Fred replied, jotting notes down.

"But he was also intensely scared of ghosts."

"Had he actually seen any?"

Ned shrugged. "He had dispatched so many men that he worried constantly that he might be confronted by one. And he didn't like my little puppets." Ned pointed to the case. "Would you hand me my valise?"

Fred jumped up and collected the valise and passed it to Ned.

"Are you there, Bill?" Ned asked.

"Be right with you, sir," came a muffled reply from the valise. Ned opened it and drew out the Buffalo Bill puppet, which he positioned on the edge of the case as before.

"How is our old friend, Wild Bill Knicknock?"

Buffalo Bill was about to reply, but from the valise an abrupt gruff voice snapped. "Don't call me that, Ned Buntline, you flowery tongued pen-pusher."

Ned reached into the case and came out with

the Knicknock puppet. It had a long straggly mustache, long hair swept back and a frock coat with big leather boots. Strapped on both hips were facsimile guns.

"You seem a mite tetchy, Wild Bill?" he asked it.

"I'll say I am tetchy, you dime store writer. You know I hate the dark and you leave me in that there valise with smiling Bill Cody there. He keeps telling me ghost stories and you know I can't abide them."

Despite himself, Fred Pond chuckled.

"Who's laughing at me?" Wild Bill Knicknock snapped, his head swivelling swiftly.

"Easy, Wild Bill," cooed Buffalo Bill. "Mister Pond here is one of the good men."

"Well, I don't like being laughed at."

Fred Pond looked contrite. "I meant no offence, sir."

Knicknock nodded. "None taken, pilgrim." He turned his head to Ned. "Reckon I'll head back then, Buntline."

"Good idea, Wild Bill. And Buffalo Bill won't tell you any more stories to scare you."

Ned stowed both puppets away and shut the valise.

"Wild Bill really hated my pre-show routines before curtain up. He thought I was making fun of him and I had to placate him many times, especially if he'd been drinking whiskey before

212

the show. One of the ways was by humouring him while we played poker. Bill Cody and Texas Jack Omohundro always obliged as they also used to like to gamble and drink a bit."

"And did the spittoon have to be—?"

"On the right of Wild Bill, yes it did. And the other superstition he had was always to have the wall behind him. He said it was so he could see who was coming towards him, but it was really just one of his superstitious foibles, I think."

Fred Pond nodded. "We all know the sad tale of his death. Of how he asked the other gamblers to move seats, but no one was willing because it could make their luck run out."

"All gamblers have superstitions," said Ned with a nod.

He struck a light to his pipe and puffed smoke at the ceiling.

"The thing is, Fred, I have felt guilty for making light of Hickok's foible as plumb superstition during one of our games of poker. I told the three scouts of the Prairie, the two Bills and Texas Jack, a ghost story about a lawman who had been cursed by an outlaw he had shot down. As he lay bleeding his last in the dust the outlaw had snarled: 'I'm going to get you when you're not ready. It won't matter where you are, or whether you're back up against a wall.' Of course, Wild Bill had his back to a wall as usual. 'Us ghosts can walk through walls, you know!'

"Then I threw my voice so that it sounded like it came from my valise, which I had left against the wall behind him: 'Put your hands up now, mister!' Of course, Hickok spun around and found himself looking at nothing but the blank wall with the valise against it. When he turned around all three of us were pointing at him as if we had guns in our hands.

" 'Caught you there, Bill,' laughed Bill Cody.

" 'Guess you oughta sit someplace else,' grinned Texas Jack.

" 'Didn't you recognize your puppet's voice. He's there in the case,' I told him."

"Did Wild Bill take it well, Colonel?" Fred asked eagerly.

Ned frowned. "He looked at me with those steely cold eyes of his and his jaw twitched. For a moment I thought he was going to draw those Navy Colts of his and finish me off then and there. But then he tossed his head back and laughed, as though it was the finest joke he'd ever heard.

"Then he picked up the valise and placed it on the card table and slowly took out one of his ivory-handled guns and laid it on top. 'Very funny, Ned. Just one thing! Don't you ever let me hear you use that Knicknock puppet on stage again. Otherwise, one of you will get your head blown off.' "

Fred stared in horror.

"So I never used him again in those shows, although I have used him on numerous occasions since then," said Ned. "But when I heard that Wild Bill was murdered in Deadwood a few years later, and that he hadn't been sitting with his back to the wall, I felt bad. Really bad." Ned's eyes glistened with tears. "So that is why I think I wrote that dime novel *Wild Bill's Last Trail* about him and put in all those details about him being superstitious and afraid of ghosts."

He crossed his legs, wincing as if he had a spasm of his old gout.

"So, where was I? Ah yes, from Philadelphia we went to Niblo's Garden in New York, where we sold out every night and people had to be turned away in their hundreds. We closed our tour at Port Jervis in New York to huge critical acclaim and I told the troupe that we should all rest for the summer."

In his own mind Ned was content that they had received critical acclaim, at least from the rapturous response of the audiences they played before. The actual newspaper critics had thought otherwise and filled their columns with disparaging criticism of him as a playwright, actor and impresario. When Ned had let it be known that he had written *Scouts of the Plains* in four hours, one critic wrote that he found it a mystery that it had taken so long. Another had said the drama was slop, the acting was execrable and that it was unlikely the play would ever be seen again. But Ned never worried what people said about him, as long as they were saying something.

"You deserved the rest, Colonel," said Fred. "It must have been a great drain on you. All that performing and having to deal with complex personalities like the Scouts of the Prairie."

"It was, Fred. Yet I was not prepared for the duplicity that followed."

Fred's eyes widened. "Duplicity?"

"I am afraid so. It happens in life. Sometimes people you trust and have done good service for, they turn on you. That happened to me. I had returned here to write and rest and plan, while Bill Cody and Texas Jack went west to spend the summer hunting.

"You see, I thought that I would make these plays into proper Wild West Shows, rather than Wild West Stage plays. I contacted a friend of mine, Phineas Taylor Barnum. You may have heard of him. He—"

"Heard of him? Who hasn't, Colonel. *The Greatest Show on Earth*. I have seen it three times."

Ned stuffed tobacco into his corncob from his yellow oilskin pouch. "In that case you know what spectacular things he gives his audiences. Gigantic marquees that he calls Big Tops, clowns, exotic animals, magicians, acrobats and so on. I conceived of doing the same, but with an entirely western theme. So I purchased the contract for a troupe of Comanche Indians from him for $16,000. Instead of having actors dressed up, I was going to use actual warriors and give people a true Wild West Show. So I contacted Bill Cody and told him of my plans to take this bigger, better show on the road in August. I arranged venues for a national tour after which I had organized a six month engagement at the Adelphi in London and was holding out for Drury Lane, which would have made a net profit of $15,000 a night."

"That would have been fantastic, Colonel," said Fred.

"It would, but then Bill Cody wrote me a letter saying that he and Texas Jack proposed to carry on with the show on their own, without me. They said that my role as Cale Durg was being jettisoned and they had created a bigger and better role for Wild Bill Hickok."

He lit his pipe. "My scouts had simply betrayed me, Fred."

Fred Pond sat upright. "Not Buffalo Bill? He wouldn't do that, surely?"

Ned sighed. "Perhaps betrayed is too strong a word, but the fact is that they had decided on their hunting trip that they no longer needed me. Wild Bill Hickok, of course was not a partner in the venture, so no opprobrium should attach

217

to him. In this sense he was, after all, only an employee."

"But you had done so much for them. You had made them famous."

Ned nodded modestly. "I suppose so. They probably felt that they had outgrown me and my meager talents."

It had indeed been an unpleasant surprise to Ned to be dismissed in such a cavalier manner, yet he was aware that it had been a pure business decision by the scouts. Neither of them had been pleased by the fact that Ned had taken the lion's share of the profits, when it had been their fame that had drawn the audiences in.

"So what did you do, Colonel? After all, you had spent all that money on the contract with P.T. Barnum."

"I did what I had intended to do, Fred. I formed the *Ned Buntline Wild West Show*. I had my Comanche warriors, and I hired two scouts and introduced them as *Arizona Frank* and *Dashing Charlie, the Texas Whirlwind*. They were based on two characters from my last story for *Street & Smith*. After training and rehearsing here at the Eagle's Nest I took the show on the road. It was a sparkling success, of course."

Ned struck another light to his pipe, which had gone out. He would never have even thought of confessing that the show was an unmitigated disaster and that without the presence of Buffalo

Bill, Texas Jack, and Wild Bill Hickok barely anyone came to see it.

"Yet I had lost my enthusiasm for it and I had an attack of gout, which forced me to come home. Bill Cody and Texas Jack had been following our progress, though. When they heard that I had cancelled further shows Bill grasped the opportunity. He built a Wild West Show based on the model I had used. And as the world knows, it has been a terrific success around the country, and he is now planning to take it to England."

Fred Pond shook his head. "I don't know how to write about this, Colonel. This could upset people."

Ned waved a hand magnanimously. "Then say nothing, Fred. It would go against my nature to be bitter and I certainly would not wish to sully good men's reputations. Perhaps merely say that after bringing them to the public attention and helping them gain their spurs, so to speak, in the acting and show business world, I was happy to wish them farewell and continued success. Say also that I remain great friends with Bill Cody and Texas Jack."

Fred whistled and shook his head. "It is a good thing that you are not the type to hold a grudge, Colonel."

Ned gave a short laugh as he leaned over and tapped his pipe out in Hickok's spittoon. "I never held a grudge in my life, Fred. It is a waste of time in my view."

He had actually never forgiven Wild Bill Hickok for running him out of town in Fort McPherson, or for threatening to blow off his or his puppet's head. That had been the reason, he thought, why he had written the hatchet job on him in his dime novel *Wild Bill's Last Trail*. He had portrayed him a bit like Shakespeare's Macbeth, a man wracked by guilt and fearful of the ghost of one-time comrade, Banquo. When you had killed as many men as the gunman claimed, Ned reckoned there would be a good chance that at least one would come back to haunt him.

As for Buffalo Bill, he planned to write another dime novel when the Wild West Show went to Britain.

Chapter 13

THE MAGNIFICENT POSSE

June 1882

Fred was incredibly busy editing *Wildwood's Magazine* over the next few months and was unable to get back to the Eagle's Nest to see the Judsons until the following summer. He had produced a series of biographical articles based on their meetings and was well advanced in his preparations to publish them in book form, once he completed the interviews.

He had been delighted to receive a letter from Ned in May 1881, containing a cutting from the announcements column of the *Stamford Mirror.*

> Eagle's Nest, Col. E.Z. Judson's home, all were made happy by the appearance of a young eagle, in good trim and as lively as a cricket. The colonel felt as jolly as a lark and has been busy writing a poem to mark this occasion. He had penned it in its entirety before he hoisted his flag against the stars. It's a boy.

Fred had sent his congratulations, flowers and a christening gift for Edward Judson Junior and thence after received glowing reports of his progress from Ned.

When he arrived for another interview in June 1882 the flag was flying high, as were Ned's spirits. Hazel Eyes was a bundle of energy, dashing about seeing to both young Edward's needs and those of her husband.

One thing that immediately struck Fred was Ned's talk of mortality. Although he and Anna Judson had coped remarkably well with the death of their young daughter Irene before Fred first met them, Edward's birth seemed to have made Ned aware that he would not live forever. After having shown him the cradle in which his one-year-old baby son rested, and having stroked the thatch of red hair that he had sprouted and was unmistakably inherited from him, Ned took his protégé up to the burial plots that he had arranged. Inside a picket fence, on a hill shaded by willow trees and overlooking the Delaware Valley Ned had laid out the plots where he imagined his family would rest. He shed a tear as he ran a hand over the memorial column to Irene with an angel upon it.

"But we all have to go sometime, Fred. It gives me some comfort to know that I'll see her again when I finally cross the last frontier and that our mortal remains will lie side by side for eternity."

Then he clapped his hands and all maudlin

mood disappeared, so that he was once again the ever-positive, optimistic Ned Buntline.

"So now, let us retire back to the Eagle's Nest and lunch before venturing into the inner sanctum to sweat more memories out of this old head of mine."

Over lunch they chatted about the things that had been occupying the news over the last few months.

"I saw that your old friend Phineas Barnum has bought a giant elephant called Jumbo," said Fred, as he cut a piece of steak.

Ned laughed. "Knowing Phineas it will be billed as the biggest elephant that ever lived." He sipped a glass of Anna's homemade lemonade and dabbed his mustache with his napkin. "Speaking of circuses, did you see that the Sells Brothers in Ohio have hired a female sharpshooter called Annie Oakley?"

Fred shook his head. "Is she as good as—" Fred began, thinking of Daisy Blanche, but immediately thought better of it when he saw Ned's eyes flash wide in alarm. "—as Buffalo Bill himself?" he asked, changing tack adroitly.

Ned gave him a half wink. "I hear that she is the best sharpshooter in the world. She outshot Frank Butler in an exhibition shoot some years back and promptly got married to him. I reckon it won't be long before Bill Cody tries to corral her.

I would have myself if I still had a mind to run a Wild West Show."

Anna smiled demurely. "Well thank heavens you haven't, Edward. Eddy Junior and I need you right here. It is time you stopped gallivanting across the country."

Fred sipped his lemonade. "I quite agree, Mrs. Judson. It gives me the opportunity to come here and carry on gathering material from the colonel."

"Gallivanting?" Ned repeated in mock indignation. "But speaking of which, have you been following the movements of Marshal Wyatt Earp and what the newspapers are calling his Revenge Posse down in Arizona?"

Fred laid down his knife and fork. "I have indeed, Colonel. I get all of the western newspapers sent directly to my office. I like to read the original articles rather than the second or third hand columns that reach us here in the East. You taught me to do that."

"A good policy, Fred. I have been following it in the *Angeles Herald*, *The Weekly Nugget* and the *Tombstone Epitaph*. Ever since the OK Corral debacle and the murder of Morgan Earp the whole thing has been absorbing news. Then Sheriff Behan formed a posse to go after Wyatt Earp, his brother Warren and Doc Holliday's posse. The last I heard was that Colorado Governor Pitkin refused to allow an extradition request on the Earps and Holliday, much to Sheriff Behan's displeasure."

Fred nodded. "Wyatt Earp does not seem to be a man to cross. He's hewn from the same stuff as yourself, Buffalo Bill and Wild Bill Hickok, I think."

Ned waved a hand dismissively. "I am just a temperance lecturer and a humble wordsmith these days, Fred. But Earp, he was always a hardcase."

Fred grinned. "I was hoping you would tell me about him, Colonel. I understand that you presented him with a weapon."

Anna gave a little laugh. "Goodness, that was just the sort of gallivanting that I was referring to. It all started with that dreadful murder." She stood up. "But if you don't mind, I'll let Edward tell you all about it later. It was quite an upsetting episode. That poor woman, Dora Hand."

After lunch Ned spent a half hour playing with Eddy Junior, while Fred Pond sketched them. Then leaving his son in Anna's care they retired to his study where Anna had left a coffee pot and cups ready for them. Fred sat opposite Ned in the big leather chair while Ned sat behind his great oak desk and poured coffees before offering his cigar box.

"Mrs. Judson sounded quite upset about your meeting with Wyatt Earp," said Fred, paring the end of his cigar with the silver cutter from the desk.

"Not about meeting Earp," said Ned, puffing his cigar into action and sliding a box of vestas across the desk. "It was the whole business of the murder of Dora Hand. Do you know of the case, Fred?"

"Not a lot, I must confess, Colonel."

Ned blew out a couple of smoke rings before continuing.

"This all took place in 1878 in Dodge City. Dora Hand was a dancehall singer and actress. A beautiful woman by all accounts and the most popular woman in town. Essentially, she was shot dead while she slept one night. Then the lowdown killer ran for it and was pursued and tracked across Kansas by an intrepid posse of five men. They wounded him, but took him alive, despite him having fired upon them. Less just men would have strung him up then and there."

Unconsciously, his hand went to his neck, as talk of hanging always brought back his own memory of the time a mob attempted to lynch him in Nashville.

"Who was the killer?"

"He was a Texas cowboy by the name of Spike Kennedy. He happened to be the son of Mifflin Kennedy, a quaker from Pennsylvania who had gone west back in the wild days and made his fortune in cattle ranching. He ran the King Ranch and the Laureles Ranch, so he had the biggest cattle outfit in Texas. He sent drives of 15,000 longhorns into Dodge City most years.

"Anyway, Dora Hand and Dog Kelley the mayor sparked it off and she stayed at his house on the outskirts of town several nights a week. Spike Kennedy had blown into town on a trail drive and thought that with his name, he ought to be able to have any woman he wanted. And he wanted Dora."

"Did he know she and the mayor were a couple?"

"I understand he was told and indeed, the mayor threw him out of his saloon *The Alhambra* when he was drunk and annoying Dora. That was when he decided to settle with the mayor, in the cowardly way he did. He fired three shots into the front of the house one night, thinking it was just the mayor who was there. Unfortunately, Dora Hand and another singer called Fannie Garretson were there, sleeping in different rooms. Apparently, one bullet went over Fannie's body, through the wall and killed Dora as she slept."

Fred blew out a stream of smoke. "A tragedy, Colonel."

"It was indeed, Fred. There she was singing to a full house one evening, then when she went to bed she could have little idea that she would never wake up again. The shot woke the town up and the murder was discovered. Poor Fannie was

227

in shock. A posse was formed and set off into the night in pursuit."

"Brave men! They could have been picked off in the dark."

"Absolutely. Those five young men were very brave indeed. For all they knew, Spike Kennedy could have had other men loyal to Mifflin Kennedy, who could have followed them in order to prevent them catching him. They figured he'd head for Texas, you see, and they'd know the trail better than the posse, so they could easily be lying in wait to bushwhack the posse."

Fred licked the point of his pencil prior to jotting notes down. "What were their names?"

"Their names were Wyatt Earp, Bat Masterson, William Tilghman, Charlie Bassett and William Duffey. When I first read about the murder and then the pursuit and capture of the suspect in the *The Dodge City Times* I knew that these five men were worthy. I felt the world should know more about them. I could make them as famous as my friends Buffalo Bill or poor old Wild Bill Hickok."

He made the sign of the cross as he said the latter name.

"I planned to tell the story of Dora Hand's murder and their manhunt of the killer Spike Kennedy in a dime novel that I would entitle *The Magnificent Posse*. More than that, Fred. I wanted them to receive a tangible reward. In my mind I saw the image of a gun that I would have made and which I planned I would present to each of these brave lawmen. They would be weapons that would mark them out as lawmen to obey and be wary of. Guns that would define the Wild West and which, together with my writing would make them famous throughout the land."

"This is the weapon that I heard you gave to Wyatt Earp?"

Ned grunted assent and tapped his cigar in the ashtray. He puffed on it to produce a bright red cone at its end. "So I settled down and designed a gun, which I felt could become a symbol of law enforcement and then contacted Richard Jarvis at the Colt factory in Hartford and ordered six. One for each of them and one for me."

"Do you have your one here in the Eagle's Nest?" Fred asked, eagerly.

"It will be around somewhere," Ned replied with uncharacteristic vagueness. He coughed. "The six guns were delivered exactly one week later, thanks to the good custom that I had given Richard for years. That and the knowledge that some good words from me in one or two of my *Beadle & Adams* dime novels could have a greater effect on sales of guns than ten gun salesmen on the road."

Fred laughed. "And who exactly is Richard Jarvis?"

"Richard Jarvis was the brother-in-law of

Samuel Colt and both have been good friends of mine. Richard took over when Sam died back in 1862. Any gun design from me was automatically inspected by Richard himself and given top priority. Over the years the Colt Manufacturing Company have produced handguns, pocket pistols, fowling pieces and carbines specifically for me."

"Can you describe the gun, Colonel?"

Ned nodded. "I called it the *Buntline Special.* It was basically a long-barreled variant of the Colt Single Action Army revolver, chambered for the .45 Long Colt cartridge. The barrel of each weapon was sixteen inches long with precision sights and walnut handles, upon which I had the name 'Ned' ornately carved. I asked for a specially tooled holster to come with each one."

"Did they shoot well?"

"I tried them all out and satisfied myself as to the weapons' accuracy and usability. Then all I needed to do was make contact and head to Dodge."

"Had you been before, Colonel?"

Ned shook his head. "Dodge City was new territory to me, although I had read so much about it that I almost felt as though I knew it. As was my custom before visiting a new town or city I sent a flurry of telegrams to various people, including the mayor, the lawman, the newspaper editor, the custodian of the best hotel and the local pastors or preachers. I usually took however many opportunities I could in order to deliver lectures on temperance, or politics if the time was right.

"Before I left I had sent and received telegraphic replies from all the recipients of my messages. The name of Colonel Edward Judson, better known as Ned Buntline has always been able to open doors. Dodge City was ready for me."

What Ned didn't tell Fred was that the real reason for his trip to Dodge City was not just to honor *the magnificent posse,* but to put a business proposition to them.

Chapter 14

DODGE CITY

Fred listened in awe as Ned recounted his trip.

"To right and left the pens were full of cattle. Maybe around twenty thousand in all. Dust, flies and as healthy a smell as ever greeted a person's nostrils, that was the scent that drifted in through the train windows as we approached Dodge City."

Ned tossed his cigar stub across his desk into Hickok's spittoon with a nonchalant and unerring aim. It sizzled as it hit the wet sand in the bottom. Immediately, he picked out a meerschaum pipe from his rack on the desk and filled it from a tobacco jar fashioned from the figurehead of a wrecked pirate galleon that he had picked up in Tortuga, and which helped him concentrate when writing his tales of buccaneers.

"The train rolled into Front Street, which ran straight through the center of Dodge City and ground to a halt with much screeching of metal. As soon as the noise stopped and the doors were opened to let the passengers descend, a brass band struck up. I kept back though, as is my usual habit on arriving by rail.

"From my vantage point I could see out, but

no one could spot me. I saw a large crowd of townsfolk had formed and at the front of them I could clearly see that a group of heavily armed lawmen and local dignitaries stood waiting. I also saw a drunk shuffle forward, drink in his hand."

Ned changed his posture, using his pipe as if it were a bottle, and with a slurred voice he went into character:

" 'Why, someone important must be coming to Dodge!' "

Immediately, he changed character and looked sideward, as if another loafer was conversing with the drunk: " 'Hear tell it's one of them temperance johnnies. Here's to him, the poor cuss, that's what I say. He won't have much custom on Front Street.' "

Ned chuckled and lit his pipe. "Passengers descended and bags, cases and trunks were handed down as the band played awkwardly on. At first they did so with pomp and enthusiasm and then hesitantly and discordantly as players missed notes as they scanned the cars in expectation. Then a group of six spinster ladies made their way down the steps, helped by a conductor and by a couple of the lawmen, who had stepped forward."

Suddenly, Ned took on the role of a lady of some refinement.

" 'Oh thank you, gentlemen,' said the first lady

to descend, a middle aged lady with wire framed spectacles, a matronly bonnet and a good quality, but exceedingly plain dress. 'We have had such an entertaining journey with the most wonderful gentleman,' she announced."

Ned laughed again as he reverted to a loafer's character. " 'You ladies found yourselves a gentleman. Must be the first one ever to hit Dodge.' "

"One of the lawmen turned and glowered in the direction of the wit, who suddenly became silent," Ned went on. "I could tell from that, the lawmen commanded respect in Dodge."

Again, as a loafer: " 'Are you ladies looking for men? Plenty of them to be found in any of the saloons along Front Street. I'd be proud to show y'all the way.' "

Ned slapped his knee in amusement. " 'Saloons! Houses of the devil, you mean!' says the lady. 'We most certainly will not be venturing there. We are the Susquehanna Ladies Temperance and Virtue League.' "

Ned was in his element, displaying a range of voices and characters. " 'You tell the man, Cordelia,' says a tall, gangly lady of indeterminate age, wearing a black toque and black widow's garb. Then turning to the dignitaries, she asked: 'Is the Reverend Harmsworth here to meet us?' "

"From the back of the crowd a reedy voice cried out: 'Here, ladies. I am here, if some of these good people would stand aside and let me through.' "

"Then one of the lawmen barked out: 'Make a passage there, folks, we have some Temperance lades coming through for the Reverend Harmsworth.' "

Ned waved his hands and assumed a serious Biblical persona. "And like Moses before the Red Sea the crowd shuffled back in two directions, making a channel for the ladies to pass through, which they did with alacrity. And as they entered the sea of folk, the crowd drew together once they were through, just as if they had been swallowed up."

Then to Fred's amusement, he put on a high-pitched preaching voice: " 'And don't forget, folks,' cried a voice from the crowd, that obviously came from the Reverend Harmsworth. 'We are having a temperance meeting tonight in the Methodist Episcopal Church at seven o'clock. Everyone is welcome and we hope maybe to have the famous Colonel Judson drop in and give us some encouragement.' "

Ned reverted to the female leader of the Sesquahana Temperance and Virtue League: " 'Colonel Judson! That was the gentlemen. . . . He was . . .' "

Ned raised his hands as if he was playing an invisible trombone. "Then her voice was drowned out as the band started up again at a signal from a tall man surrounded by a pack of greyhounds at the front of the crowd. I knew who that was and I made my entrance to much applause."

He grasped his lapels as if addressing the crowd from the carriage. "My friends, good citizens of Dodge City, I thank you. I am Colonel Edward Judson. My name may be known to you already, but if not, then you may know me better by my sobriquet of Ned Buntline. I salute you all. Then I leaped nimbly down to the ground."

Ned saw it clearly in his mind, although it was not quite as he had told it. He had leaped down, but had landed awkwardly, lost his balance as his feet rose from under him and he landed flat upon his back, much to the unbridled amusement of various well-liquored members of the crowd. The band had kept playing, but at sight of Ned's calamitous entrance they stopped at once, except for a short trombone player who had not seen the stumble. He only stopped when a fellow band player stuffed his hat over the trombone bell.

He recalled a bleary-eyed whiskey-reeking drunk at the front of the crowd leaning over him. "Well lookee here. We got us a real drunk temperance man."

Ned had winded himself and lay dazed for a moment, until several wet, licking dog tongues brought him back to reality. Yet none of this his biographer needed to know, he decided.

"I was suddenly surrounded by slobbering

dogs, jumping up at me until a sharp whistle made them desist instantly."

His mind played the memory back to him. Someone said: "Back, boys. Give the colonel breathing room." And before he knew it he was being hoisted to his feet by strong arms and dusted down by a swarm of onlookers. "That was some tumble you had, Colonel Judson," said a tall broad-shouldered man in his mid-forties. He had a thick droopy mustache, sad eyes and a doleful expression. "I am James Kelley, the mayor of Dodge City."

But to Fred: "The mayor introduced himself to me. He said he was James Kelley and he pointed to the pack of six greyhounds that obediently stood about him, wagging their thin tails enthusiastically. He informed me that people called him Dog Kelley on account of his pack of animals and that wherever he went, they did, too. I offered him my sincere condolences over his recent bereavement. I could see that he felt awkward, so I diverted attention to his dogs, of which he was inordinately proud. He told me that they had belonged to General George Armstrong Custer, whom he had served under as a scout. He had looked after them and when Custer left Fort Dodge in 1872 he gave them to him.

"Dog Kelley said he had heard that maybe I would be lecturing on the evils of drink while I was in Dodge. I had, of course, written to the local preacher, but had not arranged anything specific. I replied that it was only a possibility and that my prime reason for visiting Dodge City was to make a presentation later on to the members of the recent posse that brought in Spike Kennedy.

"The conductor handed me down my carpetbag, containing my clothes and the six Buntline Specials. Dog Kelley saw how heavy it was, but said nothing. Instead, he turned to the lawmen and said that he had explained to them all that I was visiting Dodge to do some research for a book and also to meet them and make a special presentation."

"Then Dog Kelley said, 'So, allow me to introduce you to Marshal Charlie Bassett, Assistant Marshals Wyatt Earp and Bill Tilghman, Sheriff Bat Masterson and Deputy Sheriff William Duffey.' "

Fred clapped his hands. "The Magnificent Posse!"

Ned nodded. "I said it was an inordinate pleasure to meet five of America's bravest lawmen. I pointed to my bag and told them: " 'As Mayor Kelley says, I have here the reason for my journey. If we could all perhaps retire for a libation of some sort . . .' "

"That surprised them, I think. 'A libation?' Dog Kelley echoed my word. 'Well sir, if you would care to enter my place, the Alhambra Saloon, I am sure that we can probably rustle up some milk or some sort of cordial for you.'

"That amused the crowd. Especially the lawmen. 'You are not suggesting we all drink cordial, are you, Dog?' asked Marshal Charlie Bassett, a tall, lean, clean-shaven man in a neat, but worn suit.

" 'Are we all invited?' cried out one of the bleary-eyed whiskey drinkers who were regarding me with a mixture of amusement and curiosity.

" 'If you can pay for a drink, Brooster, then you are welcome,' returned Dog.

"I raised my hand for quiet. 'Gentlemen, you are *all* invited to join us. The first drink is on myself.'

"Well you should have seen it and heard the reaction, Fred. Whoops of delight and grins of sudden affability for me, their new-found friend and benefactor flashed across the many faces in the crowd, which turned as one and beat a retreat towards the Alhambra Saloon.

"Suddenly a shot rang out and the entire crowd ducked, then spun in alarm to see the tall marshal holding a smoking weapon pointing skywards.

" 'Just making a point, men!' he cried out. 'Free drinking doesn't mean there will be a free license for rowdy behavior. There will be no fighting, no arguments and no need for any of us to lock anybody up. Now go on in a peaceable fashion and we'll all be happy.' "

Ned had raised his pipe in the air, as if it were a gun and now made a move as if holstering it. "I clapped the marshal on the shoulder and said that I had heard that the town had a reputation for being a rough place, so it clearly needed to be policed with a tough hand.

"Then Wyatt Earp, a tall young man with china blue eyes, chiseled features and a well-groomed mustache nodded. He told me that a while back some writer whose name he couldn't remember described it as The Wickedest Little City in America."

Fred Pond made a note. "I like that, Colonel. I'll put that in my article."

"Bill Tilghman, slightly built, but with an intelligent face and bright, piercing eyes hurrumphed. 'Welcome to the Queen of Cow Towns, Colonel Judson. There is a whole lot of truth in those descriptions, in my opinion. Strong drink is the main reason for that, which is why if you are a cordial drinking man, then I may well join you. I am a teetotaler, sir.' "

"That made Dog Kelley laugh. 'So says a man who was one of my competitors until recently. Bill here ran the Crystal Palace Saloon for five years.'

" 'I am a businessman,' Bill replied phlegmatically. 'I sold liquor, but that doesn't mean I had to imbibe or approve of it.'

"I applauded that and told him so. Marshal

Charlie Bassett smiled and agreed that he couldn't argue with him. Then he volunteered that he had opened the Long Branch Saloon when he came to Dodge in '72. Not only that, but he had made a handsome profit from it.

"Deputy Sheriff William Duffey was not of the same opinion. He said he'd pass on milk or a cordial, that he enjoyed a drink as much as the next man, but he disagreed that liquor was the problem. He said that it was guns that gave a town a bad name, pure and simple. That had been the cause of poor Dora Hand's death, a darned fool with a gun. Sure, Spike Kennedy had a reputation for getting liquored up, but he was dead cold sober with cold murder in his heart when he did his evil deed.

"Dog Kelley's head fell. He looked as sad as hell, I thought.

" 'Her killer walked free,' Dog said bitterly, with a vigorous shake of his head. 'It is only a pity that Bat here didn't aim a bit higher and finished him off out there.'

"Bat Masterson was a shade taller than me and of the same build. He had the look of a dandy, with a crisp, well-trimmed mustache, but with the steely eyes of a gunman. From my research I knew that he had led an adventurous life as a buffalo hunter, army scout and gambler. He had the reputation of never failing to hit his target when he had a gun in his hand. He said: 'I did what I aimed to do, Dog. I had to just stop him, so the law could take its course.'

"Dog Kelley snorted, ruefully. 'But the hell it did. The cur was acquitted, thanks to . . .'

"He said no more as the marshal's heavy hand landed on his shoulder and instead he shook his head and reached inside his vest pocket to pull out a well-chewed cigar. He stuck it in the corner of his mouth and worked it back and forth.

"The man is distraught, I thought. And that cigar has only been lit once, but not for a long time. I guessed it was his comfort cigar. I stored the fact for possible future use in a story or novel.

" 'That's why we are tight on guns in Dodge,' went on Marshal Bassett. 'Only the officers of the law are allowed to carry irons.'

"Then Deputy Wyatt Earp fixed his steely eyes on me and glanced at my heavy carpetbag. 'So as long as you aren't carrying weapons on you, you have nothing to fear from us, Colonel Judson.'

"That made me grin, Fred. I told him that I certainly had no loaded weapons about my person. Then I patted the side of my bag and said that I didn't think he'd be disappointed by the sight of the contents of my bag.

"Then he gave a lop-sided grin and said he was just joking and that I ought to call him Wyatt. He said he'd like me to expand on the contents of my bag?

"I tapped the side of my nose and said that it

was my surprise for them all and that he'd see all in good time, or my name wasn't Ned Buntline. I pointed to the crowd that was fast making its way to the Alhambra Saloon and suggested that we ought to catch up to them.

"Dog Kelley patted my shoulder and urged the Magnificent Posse to follow the crowd. He whistled and immediately the pack of greyhounds set off after the crowd, barking as they went.

"I took in the geography of the town as we went along. I've always done that whenever I've visited a place for the first time. Whether it was a forest, a swamp or a place of iniquity such as Dodge City was supposed to be, I always made it a matter of importance to know where trouble might come from and where an escape could be made to. That's a policy that I'd advise you follow, Fred. Especially if you ever plan to go exploring for books you are going to write."

Ned was ever conscious of his past humiliating experiences, such as a tar and feathering when he had a spell at snake oil peddling in Kansas as a youngster and his near lynching in Nashville, Tennessee back in '46. He vowed never to allow himself to be placed in such jeopardy again. Or at least, he'd ensure that he had better than a fighting chance of escaping with pride and body intact.

"As I walked with Dog Kelley and the five lawmen in the tracks of Kelley's greyhound pack

I took in the smells of the place, the water of the Arkansas River, the heavy, all pervasive odor of cattle and dung, the smell of mud, whiskey, tobacco and frying beef." He sighed. "I love that sense of the frontier, of a place where you can find nuggets of gold, dollars of silver or bullets of lead, all in one day."

Fred grimaced. "You mean you like to live dangerously, Colonel?"

Ned chuckled. "And opportunity, Fred. Always look for the opportunity of using the experience you get there, or someone else's experience. Store it up, because there will be a story in it for you."

"Dodge wasn't very old even then was it?"

"Nope, just a few years. Front Street had been where the town all began and consisted of a long straight and very wide street down the middle of which ran the Atchison, Topeka & Santa Fe Railroad. The rest of the road was pitted and pockmarked with wagon ruts and was even at that moment, with a locomotive about to take off, bustling with horses, wagons and people going about their business. You could see that it was a cowtown. There were sixteen saloons, a hardware store with a huge wooden sign in the shape of a rifle, appropriately painted red, boasting that it sold guns, pistols, ammunition and tinware. There was a large two storied building with stout posts supporting a canopy over the entrance and above it, the name Great Western Hotel."

" 'Is this where you'll be staying?' Sheriff Masterson asked me.

" 'Is it a good hotel?' I asked.

" 'Put it this way,' chirped in Wyatt Earp with a deadpan expression. 'If there are bed bugs in the place, they don't bite the paying guests.' "

Fred laughed. "It sounds like Deputy Earp had a sense of humor?"

Ned gave a short laugh. "He was taciturn by nature, I'd say. I reckoned he was probably as cool as ice in situations where danger prevailed. I made a mental note to work on that characteristic when I came to write my next novel, although none of the lawmen knew about my intention at that time.

"We reached the Alhambra and a couple of eager loafers were standing there holding open the batwing doors for us. Once my eyes adjusted to the light in the smoke-filled saloon I saw it was crowded fit to bust. The bar was four deep and the bartenders were dashing hither and thither serving beer and whiskey, while several saloon girls were bustling around the tables, balancing trays of drinks and fending off or responding to the attentions of the clientele.

"Anyhow, the customers were as well trained as the greyhounds and made room for Dog Kelley, the lawmen and I. Beers and whiskeys were lined up for us, alongside a glass of milk for Bill Tilghman. 'Drink up,' says Dog Kelley and that is exactly what we did.

"Everyone kept coming up to me to shake my hand, ask for a tale or two, or to have a drink on them, or even to share their glass."

Fred Pond nodded. "It sounds as if your fame had reached Dodge."

"It had, Fred. And the name often gets people talking, which is what they did. The more they drank, the more willing they were to tell me about the killing of Dora Hand and about the Magnificent Posse that went after her."

"So the lawmen were already regarded as heroes, Colonel?"

"Indeed. Unlike the killer, Spike Kennedy, who escaped the law."

"Escaped? But they caught him!"

"And he stood trial, or sort of stood trial. It was a complete sham, according to Dog Kelley and all the lawmen. Wyatt Earp was particularly disparaging about it."

"What happened, Colonel?"

Ned poured himself another coffee. "Spike Kennedy was brought back wounded and according to the posse members he confessed that he did the shooting when they were out on the prairie. He said that Dora Hand wasn't the target, though."

"That sounds damning."

"Except when they got him back to Dodge and the doctor operated and removed the bullet, he changed his mind and denied it all entirely. Well, his father, Mifflin Kennedy and a whole army of his men eventually came to town and Judge Cook ordered the trial should take place in the sheriff's office two weeks later. Mifflin Kennedy was there with his son, all bandaged up and pale as a ghost. There was a parcel of attorneys and the lawmen of Dodge, but no one else. They deliberated for two hours and then all the lawmen came out one by one. Each one more disgruntled than the other. They were all waiting there when the attorneys, Mifflin Kennedy and his son Spike came out. Spike Kennedy was free to go and all charges against him were quashed for lack of evidence."

Fred Pond stared aghast. "I don't believe it."

"Nor did any of the lawmen, but Judge Cook was adamant. Spike Kennedy was discharged with no blemish on his character. Of course, Mifflin Kennedy and his army of men drove him out of Dodge in a covered wagon. They made sure no vigilantes could attack him. They went back to Texas where a band of the best surgeons operated on him and removed about five inches of shattered shoulder bone.

"By the time I had heard all of this, the entire Alhambra Saloon were pitching in their opinions and all of us, Dog Kelley and the lawmen were pretty drunk, all excepting Bill Tilghman. I asked about poor Dora Hand and they told me that it had been the biggest funeral they had ever had in Dodge City. There were four hundred men on horses, with their sombreros off in respect as the wagon with her coffin progressed up to Boot Hill Cemetery, where they laid her to rest.

" 'I'd deem it an honor if you gentlemen could show me her grave,' I suggested. 'Of course, Ned!' they all said and the doors of the saloon were thrown open and every single person there marched out, up the street and on to Boot Hill. Dog Kelley and the magnificent posse led the way, with the greyhound pack trotting alongside them, as if realizing the somberness of the occasion.

"Her grave was just a simple mound of earth amid rocks and brush and her marker was just a simple piece of wood with her name on it and the words, *A candle in the dark, snuffed out before the light*."

"Poignant, Colonel."

"It was, Fred. So, there we were, the whole Alhambra clientele plus just about everyone else who happened to be doing business on Front Street, gathered around her grave. They were all jabbering away and no one could have any kind of a conversation. I tugged Sheriff Masterson's sleeve and asked him to get the crowd's attention. So he nodded, pulled out his gun and fired a shot in the air.

" 'Ned Buntline here would like to say a word or two,' he cried. Well of course, they all fell silent, so I jumped atop a rock to see over them all and lifted up my carpetbag.

" 'Good people of Dodge City,' I yelled. 'I thank you for showing me this cruel injustice that has seen this beautiful young woman, Dora Hand, taken from us all by the hand of an assassin. Yet we have before us these five good men, the Magnificent Posse who risked life and limb in pursuit of the man they supposed to be her killer. I won't say any more about the trial, because the law of America has spoken and I am a great believer in the law.' "

Fred Pond sipped his coffee. "I bet that went down well, Colonel."

Ned nodded. "I had to wait a few moments before the cheering and applause died down. And as it did, the crowd swelled bigger and bigger as folks from the decent parts of town came up the path to Boot Hill to see what the commotion was about, especially as a shot had been fired. I saw that the Reverend Harmsworth and the good ladies of the Sesquahana Temperance and Virtue League had joined the throng and were being allowed through for a better view."

He didn't say that he had almost fallen from the rock and was only saved by the swift action of Bill Tilghman.

"Then I said that the Magnificent Posse

deserved to be given a reward, for they were a symbol, each one of them, of what was good about America. I opened my carpetbag and produced a Buntline Special. Then I presented one to each of the posse, to unanimous applause."

" 'They look mighty fine,' said Bat Masterson, 'but how well do they shoot?' "

"Then Bill Tilghman took charge. 'Excuse me, Sheriff, but I reckon there'll be no trying out of weapons today,' says he. 'Not in Dodge City when men have been drinking.' "

" 'In that case,' says Earp, 'why don't we have a testing out of town, right now?' "

"I was still on the rock. 'Exactly my plan,' I cried. 'I have a proposition. I'll make the winner of a shooting competition with the Buntline Specials a household name. I'll make them the subject of my next dime novel.' "

"They all loved the idea, except Tilghman, who said he'd stay in Dodge and look after the town. So, before I knew it we were on our way to the livery, where a horse would be arranged for me, then within minutes it seemed that the whole population of Dodge City was riding out of town in a cloud of trail dust."

Again, Ned omitted to say that first he had to be lifted out of the dust again, having ignominiously fallen from the rock to land on his back, where he flailed about like a bull that had guzzled locoweed.

Chapter 15

SHOOTING IRONS

"We rode along the Arkansas River for some miles until Wyatt Earp, who had led the way down the trail, called a halt. He pointed to some boulders and told some of the riders to set up a series of empty bottles that they'd brought from the Alhambra. In all they set up six bottles for each of the four lawmen and six for Dog Kelley, who had been elected to take Bill Tilghman's place.

"The town folk formed an amphitheater around the area and full whiskey bottles were produced from saddlebags and shared around. I naturally took charge and established the rules. Before I did, I gave the crowd a full description of the weapon, pointing out the engraved 'Ned' on the handle and its tooled leather holster.

"As they all exchanged their gunbelts for the Buntline Special belts and holsters I went on:

" 'Each shooter will have exactly one minute to draw, aim and shoot their Buntline Special at their six targets. They will all shoot from the paced out distance of fifteen yards. First, you'll all draw straws for the order you'll shoot in.' "

Ned lit his pipe and puffed a couple of smoke

rings before proceeding. He held up the spent match as if it was a straw. "Charlie Bassett went first, then Dog Kelley, then William Duffey, Sheriff Masterson and last Wyatt Earp. I paced out the distance and drew a line in the dirt for them to use as the mark. Then I got out my watch."

As if re-enacting the event he pulled out his watch and opened it. " 'On the count of three,' I said, 'you will have precisely one minute to fire off your six shots. I'll call out when the minute is done and no shot after that will count.' "

Fred Pond sniggered, like a young kid. "Gosh, I wish I had been there, Colonel."

Ned raised his eyebrows. "You'd expect the Magnificent Posse to be crack shots, wouldn't you, Fred?"

Fred nodded emphatically.

The dime novelist continued his tale. "Well, Charlie Bassett had drunk about half a bottle of whiskey. He was pretty quick, but his aim wasn't too hot. He hit one bottle and the other bullets went whistling wide."

"How did the crowd react, Colonel?"

"Well, Dog Kelley's greyhounds didn't like it too much, and nor did the horses, but as for the humans, they made a lot of noise, a few whistles and catcalls, but not too much laughter. He'd turned and scowled at one feller, you see, as if he reckoned he'd put him off his aim by laughing."

"I guess you wouldn't want to antagonize him?"

"No, nor any less William Duffey, who had been drinking beer, so I guess he wasn't quite as unsteady in his aim. He managed three bottles, but only shot four times, because he'd had trouble drawing his gun."

"That sounds as if he could have been pretty deadly if he'd been up against another gunman," suggested Fred.

Ned nodded. "Sure he would. A bottle doesn't pose much danger, but a man with a loaded gun, that's another matter. I certainly think all of these men would be intimidating and as you know, I have had my share of looking at the wrong end of a gun barrel. Still, this was just a shooting contest. Next up was Dog Kelley. He really fumbled with his gun too, and his weapon went off, just missing his foot. He wasn't too happy, so after a curse or two he took good aim and managed two shots at the bottles, missing both times."

"Not a great result for Bill Tilghman," volunteered Fred.

"Not at all," Ned agreed. "Sheriff Masterson stepped up next and he drew his gun carefully, raised it steadily and shot, one, two, three, four of his bottles. He missed with his last two and the ricochets of the bullets from the rocks near took chunks of flesh out of a couple of watchers.

That's when I hollered at them to get back and keep a safe distance."

"I suspect that he hadn't been drinking too much," said Fred.

Ned shrugged. "Actually, I think he had, but he could clearly take his liquor. So that left Deputy Wyatt Earp. While the others had been shooting I'd noticed he'd been practicing drawing his gun. When his turn came he drew the Special smoothly and really quite fast, but then raised it deliberately so that he could use the sights to aim. He shot all six bottles in forty seconds. The crowd went crazy, shouting his name and passing the whiskey bottles around to celebrate, as if all of them had personally won the shooting competition."

"How did the others take it?"

"Like men, Fred. If anyone was at all upset it was Dog Kelley, but not because he didn't hit any bottles. He seemed genuinely upset that he had not done Bill Tilghman proud. But anyway, I told Wyatt that I was going to write not just one, but a series of dime novels with either *Street & Smith* or *Beadle & Adams* about him and that I'd begin with *The Magnificent Posse*, placing him in the lead role. So even though the others hadn't won the shooting competition, they'd still all be famous. And if the books sold well, I could write more for each of them."

"I bet they were enthusiastic, Colonel?"

"They were, Fred. The whiskey bottles went around again and we all lubricated our tonsils. By the time we remounted it was starting to get dark. As before, the four lawmen, Dog Kelley and his greyhounds and myself led the happy crowd back towards Dodge City. For a long while we rode in relative silence, all concentrating on staying in the saddle and making sure our mounts were safe. I kept looking back in the moonlight and when I saw that we had created a gap between ourselves and the rest of the party and we were out of earshot I judged it would be right to tell them about my proposition."

Fred looked blank. "What proposition?"

"To really make them famous, far beyond the dime novels that would spread their fame from one side of the country to the other. I wanted to form a real Wild West Show with them as the star attraction. I said I'd call it *The Magnificent Posse* and that we could do a re-enactment of the chase to catch Spike Kennedy."

"And what did they say?"

"To a man they were keen. Even Dog Kelley said he'd put up some money and help me to bring them to the public's attention. They could all see that the future would look good. They could be bigger by far than Buffalo Bill. There was just one proviso that Wyatt Earp made and which the other lawmen agreed about."

"What was that, Colonel?"

"We had to see what Bill Tilghman would say."

Anna Judson knocked and came in carrying Eddy Junior. It was the cue for Ned to devote some time to his son before he went to bed, which he was ever eager to do. He got out his case and to young Eddy's delight pulled out his Buffalo Bill and Wild Bill Knicknock puppets. Then followed a half an hour of ventriloquism, conjuring tricks and much hilarity from young Eddy Junior. Finally, he took him to the window and pointed outside to the spruce pole on the lawn, from whence Old Glory fluttered.

"And what must we do, Eddy?" he asked.

In answer Eddy Junior raised his hand to his brow in a semblance of a salute, which Ned immediately duplicated.

"That is right, my boy. We salute the flag."

Then to Fred: "I mean to bring Eddy up with an affection for the old flag. Once he is old enough he will help me raise it in the morning and lower it at sundown."

When Ned eventually returned him to Hazel Eyes, Fred was keen to know the outcome of the conversation with Bill Tilghman when the shooting party returned to Dodge City.

"There was a full moon, Fred," Ned said as he resumed his tale. "It had a blue tinge to it, which somehow I thought was an ill omen. Of course,

I didn't say any such thing, for lawmen, like gamblers, tend to be a suspicious group of men."

Fred nodded. He was only too aware of Ned's previous description of Wild Bill Hickok and his suspicious and superstitious nature.

"The town was quiet. Suspiciously quiet. The other saloons were open, of course, but most of their usual customers were on the trail behind us. Dog Kelley and his pack of hounds went and hitched up outside the Alhambra, while Sheriff Bat Masterson made for his office and Wyatt, Charlie and William went to check on Bill Tilghman. I bade them goodnight and after leaving my mount at the livery I headed to the Grand Hotel.

"I had just hung Old Glory out of my window when I heard rushing footsteps coming up the stairs. Instantly, I had my gun out, as past, bitter experience had taught me never to be caught unawares. Running boots in hotels at night usually meant trouble."

"And was it, Colonel?"

"It was. Charlie Bassett and William Duffey knocked on my door and called my name. I let them in and holstered my gun when I saw their alarmed faces. 'What's wrong, my friends?' asks I.

"They whispered that I had best come and so I did as quick as I could. Back in the Marshal's office they had found Bill Tilghman stripped to his underclothes, tied to a chair with a gag in his mouth. Facing him, similarly treated and gagged was the Reverend Harmsworth.

"It would have been a comical sight at any other time, Fred. But not then. Not in the Marshal's office in Dodge City, the wickedest town in the West. Both of them had been knocked out, but they told us exactly what had happened. The Sesquahana Temperance and Virtue League were not ladylike at all. Indeed, they were not even female, but were a set of low-down, thieving criminals who had been masquerading as women of refinement. They had apparently come to Dodge to rob a bank and had taken advantage of the shooting contest to first of all use the Reverend Harmsworth to put Assistant Marshal Bill Tilghman off his guard. They had distracted them somehow then when their backs were turned, they had knocked them out, stripped them and tied them up."

"Good grief!" exclaimed Fred.

"Then they had gone on a robbing spree with no one around and no law to stop them. They had robbed stores, the bank and the church. The bank teller was also found trussed up by Sheriff Bat Masterson. Dog Kelley had come running in, for the Alhambra too, had been robbed."

"So what happened? Did the Magnificent Posse go after them?" asked Fred.

Ned shook his head. "There was no clue where

they had gone. There were no witnesses, no trails. They, whoever they were, just vanished. It was presumed that they had left town calmly, individually and thence left no trace."

"So . . . So what happened?"

"Well, in the cold light of dawn, when all the drunken crowd had returned and all the businessmen found out that they had been robbed, they all sought out the law and a meeting was arranged straightaway at the Alhambra. The long and the short of it, Fred, was that Dodge City had a reputation."

Fred nodded. "The wickedest town in the West."

"No one wanted to lose that reputation. It was good for business in a bizarre way. Certainly the lawmen didn't want it to be known that they had been bested and duped by a gang masquerading as the Sesquahana Temperance and Virtue League. They felt they were victims in this. And since I had arrived on the same train as them, they somehow became suspicious of me."

Fred Pond pounded the arm of his chair. "No, Colonel, surely not!"

"They did, Fred, until I was able to persuade them otherwise. Yet they were angry and made it clear to me that they wanted no publicity about this whatever. Other than that I had come to Dodge to present the posse with the Buntline Specials, which they all thanked me for."

"What about the Wild West Show?"

Ned shook his head. "They wanted nothing to do with it and to have no further communication about it."

"And the dime novel, *The Magnificent Posse*?"

"I was advised not to write any such work if I wanted to stay healthy. So, good Fred, the next morning I left on the first train and I have had nothing to do with them ever since."

"So they passed up on their chance of fame?"

Ned pouted. "Oh I daresay they will enjoy some fame for a short while but they will never equal that of Buffalo Bill or, dare I say it, of myself."

"But they will all use the Buntline Specials? Surely they will have some reflected glory in that," Fred opined.

"Who knows, Fred. The truth is that only two of them showed proficiency with the weapon. Those were Bat Masterson and Wyatt Earp. I fear that the weapon was ahead of its time. Yet as I am sure you know, Wyatt Earp used it during the Gunfight at the OK Corral in Tombstone last October."

He neglected to tell his protégé that a week after he returned home to the Eagle's Nest he received a package containing four sawed-off gun barrels that he recognized had belonged to Buntline Specials. There was a letter written by Sheriff Bat Masterson. He explained that Charlie Bassett, William Duffey, Bill Tilghman and himself had the local gunsmith saw off the barrels of the guns to make them of useable length. Only Wyatt Earp had decided to keep his as it was, for it was a useful deterrent and a useful club for buffaloing town drunks. Whereas he clearly was able to use it as an efficient weapon, the others thought it a suicide piece, for there was a danger of not being able to remove it from the holster before a gunman outdrew them with a conventional Colt. He had ended the letter with thanks on behalf of the others, but a curt reminder that the doings of the Sesquahana Temperance and Virtue League should never see the light of day in a dime novel or any magazine associated with Ned Buntline."

Fred Pond nodded and made a note. "I shall stick to the simple version as well, Colonel. It should be enough for the reading public to know that the Magnificent Posse members each received a Buntline Special. I'm sure it will become a part of American gunlore."

Chapter 16

GONE FISHING

Fred Pond kept up his regular visits to Ned over the following three years, noting sadly how much his health had deteriorated on each occasion. His old wounds and his gout plagued him, yet he had lived with pain for so long that he was able to cope with them. When his doctor told him that his heart was failing, he tried to stir his strength and defy his condition by going fishing whenever he could, for as long as he could. Apart from that, his pen was seldom still and as his fishing trips became less frequent he did what he did best, he wrote about past trips, prize catches of salmon and trout and chance meetings with fellow anglers. Many of his tales saw print in the *New York Waverley*, while others saw light on the pages of Fred's *Wildwood Magazine* or in *Turf, Field and Farm*.

His last sketch appeared in the latter on April 30, 1886, appropriately published by Fred:

"Propped up in my invalid chair in the window of my sick-chamber, where I have battled for life for ten long weary weeks, I look out on opening leaves, bright apple blossoms, and the flashing waters of my private trout brook, while for the first time at this date for years I see no sign of snow on hillside or mountain. Tomorrow, a hundred rods will bend over bright waters within a radius of four or five miles of me, yet I must look sadly on my pet Orvis Clearwater Fly Fishing Rod in the corner, and let the split bamboo rest."

Fred saw Ned a week before he died on July 16, 1886 and penned a short eulogy to his friend and mentor, who he respected more than any man and who had urged him to carry on his mantle. This too, he published in his magazine under the title *Gone Fishing*. He hoped that Ned would approve.

"Peacefully at his home, appropriately christened 'Eagle's Nest,' among the mountains which overlook the historic Hudson, this lion-hearted, generous and remarkable man bowed his head and gave up the struggle for life. The brief message that came to us over the wire from Stamford, last Friday, announcing the death of Edward Z. C. Judson, pained us deeply, though we had been prepared for his demise by the closing sentence of his last communication to us. It is now over two years since the rugged old sportsman ascended the stairs to our office, where he was always a welcome visitor. That was his last visit, we believe, to the metropolis, although it has been my delight and pleasure to have visited him throughout these last months at the Eagle's Nest, where I first met and began to write his biography.

"History will speak of "Ned Buntline" as a dashing middy, a brave scout on the frontier, and as a fertile writer of fiction. It was as a sportsman and a brilliant contributor to sporting literature that we knew him and admired him most. The volumes of the *Turf, Field and Farm* contain many graphic descriptions of the chase and sparkling tales of the delights of angling, from his pen. I stand in awe of his gallantry, his achievements, his patriotism and above all his absolute modesty.

"God rest your soul, Colonel Edward Judson, or Ned Buntline as you are known to your millions of readers. That very last attribute, your modesty sums up your amazing life. I am sure you would have approved of me saying that, my friend. Farewell."

AUTHOR'S NOTE

When I was a youngster my grandfather used to amaze me with tales of the old days. He had worked as a ploughman, a forester, a gardener and a whiskey distiller. He told me of the Penny Dreadfuls that he used to read as a boy and of the day that he saw Buffalo Bill Cody's Wild West Show in Aberdeen, Scotland in 1904. He taught me how to spin a yarn and he stirred in me a fascination with the Wild West that has never left me. For those two things I will be eternally grateful to him.

When I became a western writer I researched the things my grandfather had told me about and I discovered that Dime Novels were the American equivalent of our Penny Dreadfuls. More than that, I discovered Ned Buntline (Colonel Edward Zane Carroll Judson, 1821–1886), the King of the Dime Novels. The more I read about him the more fascinated I became, for he was clearly a man of many parts, a man of paradoxes and a fantasist of gargantuan proportions. Sailor, soldier, scout, fur trapper, hunter, sportsman, actor, political agitator and adventurer. He seemed to have done it all. That extended to his personal life, for he was married six times, probably bigamously at times, and is said to have had several mistresses in addition.

In essence, he was a prodigious writer of popular literature who had clearly led an adventurous and very full life, and who saw no problem in aggrandizing himself and his achievements. He has been described by Jay Monaghan as The Great Rascal, which is not far off the mark, in my opinion. Yet that is not to denigrate him, for he produced a body of work that influenced and entertained millions of people. He introduced Buffalo Bill and Wild Bill Hickok to the wider world.

One of the fascinating things about him was the fact that not only did he create his own history (for example, he bestowed the rank of Colonel upon himself, although he had never been more than sergeant), but myths followed him. Although he wrote hundreds of dime novels and is credited with having more or less created the mythic Wild West, yet in fact westerns were not his main interest. Most of his output consisted of nautical tales and sporting adventures. In addition, everyone knows about the Buntline Special, the extra long Colt revolvers that he had made for Wyatt Earp, Bat Masterson and a few other famous lawmen. Yet the historical records of the Colt Manufacturing Company fail to record their order, let alone their manufacture. It seems that this myth may have been created by Stuart N. Lake, in his novel *Wyatt Earp: Frontier Marshal*, published in the USA by Houghton Mifflin in

1931 (and published as *He Carried a Six-Shooter* in the UK in 1952). William Shillingberg wrote a detailed, scholarly paper debunking this in 1976.

Ned Buntline (for this is how the world refers to him) had a willing biographer in Frederick Eugene Pond, whom we meet in this fanciful little novel about the Dime Novelist. It seems that Fred Pond accepted uncritically virtually everything that Ned told him about himself, for he truly believed that Ned should be given a place among the giants of American literature, such as Washington Irving, James Fenimore Cooper and Mark Twain. While it would be stretching things to put him in that league, it has to be said that he was a human fiction factory who produced stories loved by millions.

I have drawn on Fred Pond's biography and upon the more scholarly work of Jay Monaghan and books by others. I have taken some liberties, such as altering the supposed length of the Buntline Special, and other little snippets here and there. I have used some of his quotes to give an impression of his style and I have tried to give a sense of Ned's nature, which was generous as it was devious. He has some highly attractive characteristics as well as other less appealing attributes. He was a man who thought he had the seeds of greatness bestowed upon him, and who was quite unrepentant about embellishing his achievements and qualities. He was a rascal, certainly. A rogue, perhaps. An interesting character, definitely.

Bibliography

Cody, William, *The Life of Buffalo Bill*, Senate edition, 1994

Kazanjian, Howard & Enss, Chris, *Thunder Over the Prairie—The True Story of a Murder and a Manhunt by the Greatest Posse of All Time*, The Globe Pequot Press, 2009

Lake, Stuart N., *He Carried a Six-Shooter*, Corgi, London, 1953

Monaghan, Jay, *The Great Rascal: The Exploits of the Amazing Ned Buntline*, Little Brown and Co, Boston, 1952

Pearson, Edmund, *Dime Novels; or, Following an Old Trail in Popular Literature*, Kinnikat Press, New York, (1929) 1969

Pond, Fred E., *Life and Adventures of Ned Buntline*, The Cadmus Book Shop, New York, 1919

Reynolds, Clay, *Hero of a Hundred Fights*, Union Square, New York, 2011

Vestal, Stanley, *Queen of Cowtowns*, University of Nebraska Press, Lincoln, 1952

ABOUT THE AUTHOR

Clay More is the western pen-name of Keith Souter, a part time doctor, medical journalist and novelist. He lives and works within arrowshot of the ruins of a medieval castle in England. In 2014 he was elected as Vice President of Western Fictioneers, a post that he was honoured to serve in for two years. He is also a member of Western Writers of America, The Crime Writers' Association, International Thriller Writers and several other writers organizations.

He writes novels in several genres—crime and historical fiction as Keith Moray, Westerns as Clay More, and YA and non-fiction as Keith Souter. His medical background finds its way into a lot of his writing, as can be seen in his previous novel, *The Doctor*, in the West of the Big River series, as well as in most of his western novels and short stories. His character in Wolf Creek is Dr. Logan Munro, the town doctor, who is gradually revealing more about himself with each book he appears in. Another of his characters is Dr. Marcus Quigley, dentist, gambler and bounty hunter.

If you care to find out more about him visit his website: http://www.keithsouter.co.uk

Or his blog http://moreontherange.blogspot .co.uk

Or check out his regular contribution about 19th Century Medicine on the Western Fictioneers blog.

| Books are produced in the United States using U.S.-based materials | Books are printed using a revolutionary new process called THINKtech™ that lowers energy usage by 70% and increases overall quality | Books are durable and flexible because of Smyth-sewing | Paper is sourced using environmentally responsible foresting methods and the paper is acid-free |

Center Point Large Print
600 Brooks Road / PO Box 1
Thorndike, ME 04986-0001 USA

(207) 568-3717

US & Canada:
1 800 929-9108
www.centerpointlargeprint.com